All the Spangled Host

All the Spangled Host

John A. Ryan

THE LILLIPUT PRESS
DUBLIN

Published in 2015 by
THE LILLIPUT PRESS
62–63 Sitric Road, Arbour Hill
Dublin 7, Ireland
www.lilliputpress.ie

ISBN 978 1 84351 661 3

10 9 8 7 6 5 4 3 2 1

A CIP record for this title is available
from The British Library.

Set in 12.5 pt on 16.5 pt Centaur by Marsha Swan
Printed in Spain by Grafo

Contents

All the Spangled Host

Mary of the Angels

In the sunny porch, Sister Agnes was watering the blue cinerarias, while Sister Colette trotted after her, chattering. The two old nuns, engrossed in their conversation, did not even glance at Sister Mary of the Angels as she hurried past. She caught a phrase or two: 'The boys adore him ... Quite extraordinary ... Just because he's an athlete ... physical ...'

Old gossips, she thought as she opened the door.

There was no need to ask who the athlete was; everyone in this small town seemed to be talking about the newcomer. Angels remembered things she had overheard in class: 'Did you see him in yesterday's paper?' 'He's on the Munster team, too.' 'I saw him playing football with the boys.' She recalled the envious squeals of the other girls on the morning when Lily Grant, with smug triumph, showed them his signature in her autograph album. Fr Landers, when he came visiting to the convent, spoke constantly about 'our new teacher', and seemed to think he had done something wonderful in appointing the young man as assistant in the boys' school. As though, Angels reflected, being a good footballer was more important than being a good teacher. Maybe to a Kerryman it was.

She went out and along the path beside the grass. 'Physical?' No. She didn't think so. Hero-worship was not a physical thing. Rather it was almost a religious feeling; it was the yearning that was in every heart for the ideal.

The path brought her to the high stone wall with its wooden door, the top of which curved to a point. She lifted her hand to the latch and then stopped and turned to look back at the quiet garden she had just walked through without seeing. A smooth lawn that lifted and curved, a seat in the shelter of the trees, birches and yellow daffodils. 'Sister Agnes's garden,' so Reverend Mother said. 'A triumph of patience and imagination.' Long before Angels was professed, even before she came here as a boarder, Agnes was working on this, and every stone so patiently removed, every bucketful of soil so laboriously carried there ('It was once a farmyard, you know'), all was Agnes' work. A very patient and gifted old lady. 'And not,' Angels rebuked herself, 'not an old gossip.'

She opened the door and went out into the paved area in front of the church. The senior girls, instead of going into the church, were standing in groups. There was a suggestion of pointing ... it was only their eyes ... and she heard clearly, 'Isn't he gorgeous?' She looked quickly. A tall lithe figure, fair-haired, was leading the boys in by the church-gate. She should not have looked, she dragged her eyes away. 'Come along, girls,' she said, confused, the small guilt making her voice sharp. There was some sniggering and she thought she heard,

4

'... just suit Angels.' Upset by their behaviour and further upset because she knew she was blushing and that they might notice, she rounded them up and marched them through the gloom of the porch and they clattered noisily to their places. How graceless they can be at that age, she thought, and then she smiled a little when she remembered that she herself was not much older.

She stood under the organ-loft, her gloved hands on the top of the pew before her. There was no hurry really, it was not eleven yet and she would wait here until she had regained her composure.

Old Mr Malone came in. He would soon be retiring, and then she supposed the young footballer would replace him. He smiled at her vaguely, and she was sure that he had no idea who she was or what her name was, though he had been meeting her now for the past two years.

But Mr Malone, as he went down the side-aisle, thought briefly: 'Mary of the Angels. What a lovely name. And what an odd, remote little girl she is. They join at sixteen or seventeen or so, and from then on the personality atrophies, like a half-opened flower touched by frost.' Then his thoughts went back to the problem that had been worrying him, this new young man who had so captured the imagination of the children but who was so impatient in the classroom and was already in trouble for striking one of his pupils in a fit of temper.

Angels watched the boys filing in. Didn't they move so much better than girls? Was it their build, or because they played games, or was it self-consciousness on the girls' part?

They settled into their places and even their animal spirits seemed to be subdued by the quiet and peace of the church. One hoped it was due to reverence and religious feeling.

The church clock struck eleven. At this time on the first Thursday of every month the children of both schools came to confession. It was a peaceful hour, a complete contrast to school-work. The church seemed to her to absorb all these people and impose on them its own stillness, its own character of prayer and devotion. Sunshine slanted dustily from the high windows, bringing muted rich colours to the floor. Even the sounds, she thought, had a quality of remoteness so that they hardly disturbed the silence: whispers; a shoe knocking against timber; the strange clicking noise made by the weights and chains of the church clock that always made her think of coins falling into a metal bowl. Mr Malone and Fr Landers were having an earnest unheard talk near the pulpit, the headmaster gesturing with his hands, Fr Landers listening with his head bent and turned to one side. They seemed miles away, like figures on a far-off horizon. Beyond the bright and dusty curtains of sunlight, she could just make out the gleam of brass on the altar and the floppy heads of white chrysanths.

Someone had stopped beside her. Without looking, she knew who it was. She felt rather than saw the height and bulk of him, and looking down she saw the powerful fingers splayed on the pew-top. Fascinated, she could not take her eyes away. She could see the hairs quite clearly. Short golden hairs. They made the hands somehow terribly male. Quickly she snatched up her own hands. Now he turned to look back and his arm touched hers. She felt the heaviness of his shoulder touch the slimness of hers.

Her heart thumped. What was the matter with her? She must go down to the front of the church – but to do that she would have to go around him. She stayed where she was, her breath coming quickly, and she felt the blood flooding her cheeks.

Her prayer-book! Yes! Her fingers trembled as she opened it. Prayer before a crucifix ... Prayer against temptation ... The little book fell to the floor and as she stooped, quickly and in great confusion, to retrieve it, he leant down in one cat-smooth movement, she stumbled, then he was holding her elbow and handing back her book and she saw the blue eyes and heard the murmur of his voice. Thank you she tried to say and failed and turned and found her way out into the dim coolness of the porch, her face on fire, the hammering of her heart hurting, the great sunny doorway of the church before her now. She turned from it and ran in the open doorway of the choir-loft and fell panting against the curving stair, her forehead against the cold metal ... O Blessed Michael who with flaming sword didn't guard the gates of paradise ... And as her heart slowed again her tears began to fall.

The Heel of the Hunt

'**B**atty dear,' said Lady Catherine, 'you will have a little drink, won't you?'

He slipped an arm around her waist and ran with her up the steps. In the doorway he stopped and put a big hand on each of her hips and grinned at her. She noticed that he smelt pleasantly of horses.

'Tiddy, it's no wonder that Sam is fond of you,' he said. 'You know exactly what a man needs.' He grinned again. 'Come in here behind the door with me –'

She escaped from him, laughing, a bit out of breath, and she was thinking not for the first time of the paradox that was Batty Harrington: a fine big man, any girl's fancy, and a charmer too when he liked, and yet the worst marriage risk in Ireland. She thought of Maggie then, and that made her sigh, not for Maggie of course but for Batty.

Her husband was placidly handing out drinks to the early-comers.

'A little something for Batty, Sam.'

Sam poured out a large Paddy and handed it across the table.

'I'm glad you came, Batty,' he said. 'I wanted to see you. Are you going to Punchestown?'

'Of course I'm going to Punchestown. I'll ask Bord Bainne to milk the cows.'

'That's all right,' said Sam. 'I'll send Peter Redmond over to do your cows, and the two young fellows can manage here. I suppose Wigeon will be able to come?'

'Is he not here?' asked Batty, and a little cloud that had been on the fringe of his consciousness grew just a little bigger and darker.

'No. Hasn't come yet,' Sam replied, and then maybe realizing that Batty was disappointed, he added, 'Won't be much good to us today with that damaged wing, but he'll surely put in an appearance later on.'

The meet at Coolgard House was notorious for being late in moving off. Sam Wilson loved hunting but he was incurably hospitable and this always delayed the start. It suited Batty, because Skoury wasn't able for a long day of it, not under Batty's weight. Today, however, things started early, probably due to the efforts of their new joint-master.

The day was cold, cloudy and dry. The wind was from the east. The horses' breath steamed as they moved down the drive. Well, a good hunting day, at any rate. Wigeon hadn't come, but with an arm in a sling, why should he? He'd probably be at Coolgard when they got back and they could have a jar together. Batty sniffed that keen air and shivered, and it was not because of the cold, but the old primeval excitement and expectancy

9

that never failed, never had failed in twenty years or more. He looked around and found Robin McCormick close behind him. 'Morrow, Robin. Good class of a day.'

''Tis a good day, Bat, however long 'twill last. 'Twill snow before night. And I don't like that one bit. Have you any hay you could sell me?'

'I'll tell you that on Patrick's Day,' and he looked at the grey sky and started mentally counting bales.

Out ahead, Tim Kelly was swearing fluently at his hounds, his blue-jowled head pushed well up into a bowler, while towards the rear of the hunt, sure enough, there was the new joint-master, Mrs Ruth Knatchbull, all the way from Pennsylvania. MFH. Mistress of Foxhounds. She was egging somebody on. She was an enthusiastic egger-on. What a face! What a moustache! Yoicks!

He began to think he shouldn't have had that last Paddy, but it was because he'd had to drink it off in a hurry. These Americans had no idea of the value of time. These cursagod ditches! They sound all right in lyrical things that you read in *Horse and Hound*. The Quorn. The misty morn and all that. The Quorn, the Quorn, the lusty Quorn. One of these days he'd be found dead in one of these gripes. A glorious death, but wet and uncomfortable.

They were taking the same route they had taken on that Stephen's Day, when was it? A year ago? Two? The day he had grounded Sarah in Hearne's barn. Yoicks! He snorted with laughter. The horn, the horn, the lusty horn!

And there it was now, as Kelly blew his hounds out of the home covert, which in courtesy they had to draw but which wasn't worth wasting much time on.

He found old Canon Pettigrew beside him when they stopped near the Cashel road.

'They're slow in finding,' said the Canon. 'It's because of all the rain.'

Batty tried to recall when they'd had all the rain, but as well as he could remember it hadn't rained for a fortnight.

'You'll catch a cold, Canon. What happened to your hat?'

'I'm afraid it must have fallen off,' he said, peering around uncertainly.

Good job his head is screwed on, thought Batty. It was never easy to know just how conscious the Canon was.

Hounds were working at a high place of briars and rusty bracken. Nolan's *lios*. They'd get nothing there only fairies. Tim Kelly must have been thinking the same way. He shook up his hounds and took them smartly away, moving north towards the higher ground. After drawing a blank at Jacobs', they tried Hogan's knock, and at once got results. A loud blast on the huntsman's horn was answered by the music of the hounds. Rounding a corner, Batty nearly ran into the Canon, who was standing in his stirrups, staring in the opposite direction to that taken by the pack and shouting at the top of his voice, 'Gone away!'

It's his brains, thought Batty, and laughed, and shouted, 'This way, Canon!'

He took the longer way round Burke's to avoid the stony lane and he remembered another day when Wigeon, after being similarly hindered by the Canon, had come up to them, red-faced, spluttering, 'That blunderin' old eejit, Canon Pettigrew, got right across me, nearly had me off. Silly old bugger, always gettin' in the way, with his owl's head on him, and that stupid-lookin' animal of his like a cross between a jackass and a ... a ...'

'Come, Mr Stewart,' Lady Catherine had interposed. 'You have a wonderful flow of language but you do know that poor Canon Pettigrew doesn't see very well.'

'He's well able to see what I put on the plate of a Sunday,' Wigeon had said, winking at Batty. Wigeon's rages produced more fun than fury and never lasted long.

The gallop came to a stop beyond Burke's when they lost their fox at the little stream that runs down into Minaun. They climbed the farther slope and reached the level again through an open gate. He mopped his face with a large white handkerchief and then carefully wiped Skoury's neck and tickled him behind his ear and whispered to him as they moved slowly across a ploughed field.

Now who was that on Robin's gelding? A likely-looking bit. It must be one of Robin's daughters, but they couldn't be that age yet. What a thigh! He raised his cap very civilly.

'Some idiot drove his sheep right across the line in front of us,' she snarled. It was one of Robin's daughters all right. She sounded just like the gentle Pauline.

'Some of these country fellows haven't a clue,' he said mildly.

'Peasants!' she hissed. She had a luscious mouth, for all that. Like her mother, Pauline Kerr.

Peasants they used to be, now they're all gentlemen; Robin no less, himself no less, and this strapping wench with the pouting red lips a peasant's daughter, God bless her. Fine girl you are, steer clear or Robin might want him to marry her. What she didn't know — how could she? — was that the peasant with the sheep was young Dave Burke whose father, Dave, had grounded Pauline in the old days. That, of course, was before Pauline sobered up and married Robin.

Whoa, there, Skoury! Must let out that iron a bit, his left leg was hurting again, memento of Killatiarna, by God that was a day and a half. He swung to the ground and then remembered his flask.

'Batty, is something the matter?' It was Lady Catherine. Me fly is open, he said, but not out loud, you didn't say things like that to Lady Catherine. He went to slip the flask back into his pocket, and then thought, Hell! Why?

'Would you like a little drop to warm you?'

'Why, thank you, Batty.' She was a good sport. She didn't really want it and he suspected that though she put the flask to her mouth she drank none. What a woman she must have been in her day. She still had two of the finest legs in the county.

But as they waited together near the Lacken covert, he was thinking of another similar encounter, not with Lady Catherine but with Maggie.

'Have a jorum, Maggie. 'Twill tighten the elastic in your knickers.'

'You're deplorably vulgar, Batty,' she had said, coming up close beside him and digging her knee into him.

'I know, I know. It's the way I'm made. But I'm irresistible to women,' and he had looked down at her grinning.

'Are you sure you mean irresistible? Are you sure you don't mean irresponsible?'

That wasn't his line of country at all, so he had only grunted and said, 'Don't drink all that.'

He remembered, however, the way she had persisted. 'You really do believe that. You really believe you're the answer to any maiden's prayer. And that's the rock you'll perish on, Batty.'

She had said it in such a way that from that day on he had been a bit scared of her and had never felt as free and easy with her as before.

It was the hounds giving tongue in a very businesslike way that jerked him from his reverie.

'They've put up something,' said Lady Catherine, and sure enough when they rounded the covert, there was the pack stretching out up a half-ploughed stubble. Batty yelled 'He'll have to give us a run. He's headed away from the hill,' and at that moment he caught a glimpse of the fox on the wintry horizon just before he disappeared. They swept on and were soon labouring up that stubble. He could feel the lift and thrust of Skoury's shoulders as he leaned forward, and then he gave him a breather as they stepped up a stony lane towards the top, joined now by several other riders. Then out again into the open, and a glorious run began, right the full length of Benire valley, Lady Catherine thundering along beside him, away out in front hounds at full stretch. Kelly struggling to keep in touch, he could see no one else, the wind cold and cutting on his face. There really was nothing in the whole world to compare with it after all.

Their fox took them straight across the muddy place at the bottom of Jefferies' fields. The pack managed it with difficulty, but of course it wouldn't hold a horse.

'Keep up,' he yelled at Lady Catherine. 'The gap is in a wicked state. You'd go to the elder in it,' and they kept along the higher level and jumped the stream farther on. Glancing back he saw that at least three of the others were stuck at the muddy place and he laughed loud. 'The old dog,' he shouted. But Lady Catherine was now losing ground and he was on his own. Not quite. Two others were off to the right – one of them was surely that English fellow, the other looked like Tom Loughlin – but they seemed to have come across by Barnakillen lane and hadn't come over the hill at all.

He and Tim Kelly had it all to themselves and at the end of that great run, one of the best he thought that they'd ever had, he was still there when they killed, right under Bawncreea wall.

Very small their brave fox looked now, that had been so full of running and of guile so short a time before. He had been beaten by less than two hundred yards for the break in the wall and the safety of Bawncreea wood.

Tim and Batty shook hands solemnly. Respect for hard riders and contempt for lesser men was in that handshake. Then Tim took his tired hounds away towards Bawncreea cross. The light was beginning to fail. Batty headed for Coolgard, hacking first along the level, but then walking where he met the long rise to the main road.

Now on the long trudge back, he felt elation draining out of him. Why he should think of Maggie again he didn't know. She should be here. Instead she was likely out with the Kildares or whoever hunted up in that part of the country. Who would have thought she was all that interested in getting married? And that bit of a fellow, a lightweight, hardly any taller than Maggie herself, he'd never be able for her. 'Capable of producing hunters,' the phrase jumped, oddly, to his mind. If any woman was calculated to produce high-quality stock, surely it was Maggie. But whoever was getting hunters on Maggie now, it wasn't Batty.

He shook his head as if to shake away the idea. Well, there were others. There was that viperish young filly with the pouty mouth, Pauline Kerr's daughter. Too young! Too young for you! Now what put that thought in his head? He was only forty-three, going on — what? Next week? — well, not forty-four yet. But she's only eighteen or nineteen. Oh hell, if they're big enough, they're old enough.

There was a light already in Flanagan's, one of the famous oil lamps; with windows a foot square their lighting-up time was bound to be early. Anything except temptation, he thought, and going round to the back he left Skoury in the stable. 'Five minutes, Skoury,' he said.

He took his drink over to the fire and sat down in the welcome warmth. At the other side sat a small man drinking a large stout. That was Tom Callaghan, spoiled poteen-maker, grave-digger and handy man.

'Good morrow, Tom.'

Tom looked up slowly and surveyed him from heel to head.

'Jaysus,' he said. 'Comfort me in me last agony,' and went back to his stout.

Not an easy man to talk to, reflected Batty.

After long silence, Tom asked, with heavy sarcasm, 'Well, did yiz ketch anything?'

'What have you against the hunt crowd, Tom?'

'Idlers. Idlers and their fancy women. Tell the truth of you, though, Batty, you were never an idler.'

'And no fancy women either,' said Batty, and then was sorry he'd said it. 'Did you ever hunt, Tom?'

'Oh ay. Isn't that what killed all belongin' to me?'

'It's a thing that grows on you. If you once follow hounds on a good horse, you'll never again ask for any other sport.'

'I must saddle the jennet,' said Tom sourly.

Uncheered by his stop at Flanagan's, he set off on the last half mile. Near Fitzgerald's he saw a hound that looked very like a straggler from the pack. It wasn't like Tim to lose one of them. Batty whistled him, but the animal loped away.

As Coolgard House came in view he was reminded of the last time they'd had the Hunt Ball there. A night and a half! A night till morning! He remembered sitting on the broad carpeted stairway with Wigeon beside him, glasses of malt in their hands, studying the legs of the women who went up and down the stairs, and exchanging pleasantries with them all. Wigeon wasn't long back home after a trip to England with some beef group and he spoke as though he had managed to escape from something he never wanted to see again.

'We don't know how well off we are in this country. Do you know what? The first time I asked for a drink over there they had to search the house to find a bottle of whiskey. They had Scotch of course, but I'm talking about real whiskey. And when they found it the girl in the bar poured out a little drop and 'clare to God it hardly wet the bottom of the glass.' He looked mournfully at Batty. 'Do you remember when we were goin' to school they told us an atom was the smallest thing that could hould be itself? Well, that's not true. The smallest thing in the world is the English measure of whiskey.'

'I'd believe you,' said Batty, but he wasn't giving all his attention to the conversation because he could see Maggie almost directly below him and with that low-cut dress she was wearing he could look down between Galteemore and Slievenamon. She looked up and saw him and made a puss at him, and at once he stood up and went down to her, ignoring Wigeon's 'What ails you?' and leaving his whiskey on the stairs, because whiskey can be replaced but opportunity can't.

He shook his head again. That was all water under the bridge now.

At Coolgard House he said, 'I'll put you in your box, Skoury.' He gave him a quick rub-down, fastened a blanket on him and left him munching in his box. He would just have a quick look to see if Wigeon had come, then he must get on home.

Going up the steps, he felt the tiredness and a twinge of pain in his hurt leg. He stopped for a moment and looked across the trees at the lowering sky, and a snowflake drifted down and landed on his sleeve. Must get home, he thought. He went into the hall, which was pleasantly warm after the raw air outside. A pert and plump girl wearing a little white cap and a little white apron was crossing the hall with a tray.

'Kitty, is Willie Stewart here?' he asked her.

'No, sir.'

He hadn't really expected him, yet he felt keenly disappointed. It wasn't his way to show it, however.

'Begod, Kitty, you're puttin' on weight. It looks well on you, though,' and he made a rawm at her.

'Stop, Batty. I mean sir. You'll make me drop all the glasses.'

He was standing near the garden window and he could see the sullen clouds darkening outside. He found himself wishing that he hadn't to go home; here there were lights and warmth and people. For a while he stood watching the flakes of snow that fell against the glass and melted, and his thoughts were bleak.

Well, there was work waiting to be done, animals to be fed and seen to, and these things wouldn't wait. He turned heavily towards the door. But now Sam had seen him and came over.

'Batty, I didn't see you come in. What will you have? I know you can't stay, but have some little thing before you go.'

Batty hesitated. Then he said, 'I'll have a drop of Rémy Martin,' but it wasn't because he wanted it. Nor was it camaraderie that made him say it. It was, rather, a kind of terror. It was something very like defeat.

Chapel Street

Paulie swept into Chapel Street at four miles an hour almost. Then he slowed down. His forklift whined eagerly; it was going well; it paid to look after a machine. He slowed down because he liked Chapel Street and it is a good idea to do something slowly when you like doing it. There were always things to be seen here that were worth thinking about. And you might catch a glimpse of Kate. Also he was carrying two long planks crossways and you couldn't rush that kind of job.

Chapel Street is maybe a hundred yards long, or more, and it would take him, oh — say, one long minute, maybe two, to reach the far end. But he wasn't going that far. At the far end, the street went under an archway and then out in front of St James's, but before he reached that he would turn right and go into Wattie Moore's timber-yard and there he would delicately lower the two heavy planks he was carrying, so delicately that they didn't tilt, so both ends hit the ground at the same time and the planks were undamaged, and no one could do that like Paulie could.

He watched the planks to judge if they were correctly centred and balanced. Then he looked along the street. It was almost empty. The curve of the street meant that he couldn't see the timber-yard, or the arch, but he could see St James's high above the other roofs. The sun had disengaged itself from the tower and was peering into Chapel Street over one of the sloping side-parts of the church. The houses on one side were warming up in the sunshine. The houses on the dark side crouched and made themselves small; the sunlit houses bloomed and swelled and stuck out their chests.

Halfway along, the two Coppingers had put up a small scaffolding, three long planks white with mortar and lime and paint, laid across two barrels. The small Coppinger was fussing around with pots of paint while the big heavy Coppinger, the uncle, was climbing slowly and heavily but steadily up a little ladder propped against one of the barrels. White coats, white paint, whitey lime-covered planks.

The Schooner's wife — which one? — was kneeling on the footpath outside her front door, with bucket and scrubbing brush, and Paulie saw her plumpy white knees as she bent forward. He was a well-brought-up young man and he looked away. Then he risked another quick look just to see what she was wearing, but no luck this time, she was squatting back on her hunkers, squinting up at each of the neighbour's windows in turn. It *was* a risk, too, he could go to hell for doing that. And if the Schooner caught him at it Paulie wouldn't live to go to hell.

Next was Miss Lark's house, Lavender Cottage, neat, shuttered, prim, shut up tight at door and window as though on guard against anything that might threaten her spinsterhood.

A bottle of milk stood red-capped on the step with its back firmly against the door-jamb. Not a welcoming house. He tried to look in the upstairs window but he wasn't quite high enough and besides the Venetians were slanted against him. She was not a generous lady. Not like the Schooner's wife, who really lived more in the street than in her house and was always doing something worth looking at.

The longer plank was dipping slightly at the left end. A subtle feint towards the right and then a little swooping lift the other way put everything in order again. Oh, it was intoxicating to have such power and such judgement in using it. He adjusted the jaunt of his cap; he hawed on his finger-nails and polished them on his lapel.

The house beside Miss Lark's was unoccupied. Over the door and the big window you could still make out Pringle, High Class Grocer. It still belonged to Pringle probably, if he hadn't drunk it, too, along with the tea and the sugar and the flour and the butter, till the collar came over his head from drinking and he had to be led away to St Leonard's for the Brothers to do a job on him.

Sun was warm now, although it was autumn time. Up in the blue sky above the church tower the rooks were tumbling and playing and cawing, and on Canon Burke's red-brick wall the pears plumped indolently and soaked in the heat through their russet skins and turned it to sweetness. It was a ripe, contented time of year.

Opposite Pringle's, in the shadow, lurked Peejay's bicycle repair shop. The door was closed – was it? When it was open it looked closed, when it was closed it looked no different. It opened only two inches anyway at any time, though you could squeeze another inch against the tangle of old crocks and older crocks tied it seemed in an inextricable knot with cobwebs and chains. The window beside the door had never been big, but over the years its area had been encroached on by wheels and mudguards and hubs and other nameable or unnameable bits of machinery; walls, too, once white-washed, had acquired a time-coating of dust, and from every nail hung wheels that looked like large spiders' webs and webs that looked like wheels. The high ceiling could not be seen, it was in utter darkness and from this a long furry flex came down and held a yellow glowing bulb. Under this light Peejay worked, the hub of this slightly buckled wheel of industry, the arch-spider from whom radiated every web and spoke and cable, every loop and parabola. Here he worked in dust and silence and concentration and great content. All around him sprawled his stock in trade, his spare parts, his tools; before him knelt in reverence his patient, for he was a bicycle-doctor, almost a bicycle-psychiatrist. He had once been a champion cyclist (hard to believe now) and he had taught himself his trade, and probably no one knew more about the innermost workings maybe even the innermost thoughts of bicycles. If you brought him a bicycle to mend you had to prop it against the outside wall, no room to squeeze it in the door, no room inside, and Peejay said, 'Lave it there, boy', and when you returned, it was propped against the outside wall but now perfected in smooth and shining unction, no creak or squeak no grit or jerk marred its cyclical excellence of motion.

How did he bring a bicycle in? or out? You must not worry about things like this. Where there is an artist there will be mysteries.

Paulie could see no bulb glowing and this was how he knew the door was closed.

When you met Peejay in Flanagan's at night he was a different man, talkative, his concentration unscrewed, telling big improbable lies and liable to break into song in a floriated rococo style. Ah sweet mystery of life.

Flanagan's was quiet. It ought to be open. Paulie couldn't see the church clock because the sun was in his eyes. But it wasn't open. Doll was no early riser. He noticed there were bottles and glasses and puddles of porter still on the counter.

But the house that dominated Chapel Street was Wattie's. It was taller than the others and its creamy painted walls swelled and boasted in the sunlight, and its two arched doorways (because it was two houses once upon a time) were like two eyebrows raised.

Wattie matched his house. He was the big man here. He owned half the street, and two yards, and land outside the town, and that is good progress for a man who, when he started to climb, had neither a ladder nor as much land as he could rest it on.

You ought to see him when he has a few drinks taken, and the more he drinks the further he pushes the hat back on his head and the louder he talks. Paulie recalled last night: 'The first place I ever worked was for Phil Hannigan of Currahaglash. He was a kind of a distant uncle of mine. He had several men workin' on the farm then and he was known far and wide for dietin' the men on herrin's. "Very good for the brain," he used to say.'

'That's where you should have stayed, Wattie,' said Peejay. ''Twould have been the makin' of you.'

'I couldn't stay there. The herrin' bones had started to come out through me waistcoat.'

In fact he had run away from Hannigan's and joined the navy. And he swore that he had sailed the seven seas and that there wasn't as much herrin's in the whole lot of them as there was in Hannigan's dairy.

'We were cruisin' wan day in the Caraybian Sea, and here wasn't there a shoal of herrin's passin' by, all blue and shiny with the sun and the spray on 'em, and wan herrin' puts up his head and he says, "Excuse me, sir. Oh, 'tis Wattie Moore. Wattie, am I on the right road for Hannigans of Currahaglash?"'

And Wattie had pushed back the hat and looked around, daring them.

It was talk like that, and people like that, that made Flanagan's still the best house in the town.

As for that story, Paulie would have been the last man to contradict him, but it was hard to believe, wasn't it? How could that herrin' possibly know Wattie? Not denyin' that he was a well-known man. All the same…

Sometimes people who didn't know him felt sorry for him when they saw the drooping shoulders and the long sad face. This was very foolish of them and it didn't harm Wattie's business.

Old Carraway's car was parked outside. Didn't leave much room, did it? Plenty of room for it inside the wall, but he was too lazy to get out and open the gate. Too high and mighty, just because he was a solicitor. He was probably at his breakfast now. Himself and Kate. Where did he find Kate? She must be twenty years younger than him, at least, and as plump and juicy as he was withered and dry. Maybe he did get her in a raffle, like Peejay said. She made Paulie think of a ripe plum. She was dark and luscious like a Victoria that is half of a long Autumn day too ripe, dark and smooth and bursting with life and lusciousness and sugar. Supposing, Paulie wondered, supposing someone shook the tree?

Well, if he got his motor car scratched it served him right for parking it in a narrow place. Still, he squeezed the forklift past it cautiously. Old Carraway was a bad man to fall foul of. Damages.

Dan Tierney was delivering milk to Gorman's, walking carefully on his big flat feet, nodding and smiling and whispering to himself. He put two bottles on Gorman's step and chuckled as he straightened up. Big joke! It looked to Paulie as though he had a power of funny stories that he hadn't told himself before.

He looked again at the pears that showed amber and russet above the Canon's wall. He could reach them all right, but still … You wouldn't know about the Canon. Excommunication. Paulie had no idea what that involved but it sounded pretty alarming.

The big heavy Coppinger was skilfully placing his foot on the third step when Paulie's forklift struck one of the barrels and the whole lot went flying. The three white planks went three different ways. One went through Gorman's open window and knocked a geranium that was inside and there would be murder about that because she didn't like having things spilled on her carpets. One barrel stayed upright, the other rolled slowly along in front of Paulie. The big heavy Coppinger was left lying on his back on the footpath with his arms and legs in the air.

Paulie whined on, watching his own two planks, watching that cursed barrel, until, with relief, he saw it change direction and trundle onto Canon Burke's cattle grid and stop there, an orange tom returning home after victories skipping nimbly out of its way.

But somebody was shouting. He realised the shouting was at him, and then the small Coppinger, the nephew, jumped up behind him on the forklift.

'You dirty rat!' he yelled, beating Paulie on the top of the head with his paintbrush. 'You dirty yellow rat!'

He must not let this noisy fellow upset him. Wasn't it a good thing he was wearing his cap? He turned a beautiful turn in the yard door without stirring his two planks and he thought, Was there another forklift driver in the County who could do that? Once inside the yard, he executed one of his best routines, a sudden stop which dropped the planks on the ground in front of him and an even more sudden jerk forward which threw the noisy painter into the pile of sawdust that always lay to the right of the door, while Paulie sent her full speed out the second door into the Main Street. As he cleared the door he leaned back and slammed it shut. Safer.

It *did* seem to Paulie that the world was a risky kind of place, full of dangers. Physical and spiritual. And financial. A young man had to be on his guard always.

But his day had begun well. If Wattie didn't give him that extra £2.50 he'd look for a job somewhere else. There were builders and fellows going mad looking for good forklift drivers, and Paulie couldn't deny that maybe he was the best forklift driver in the world.

Passing the archway he took a look down Chapel Street. The big heavy Coppinger was still on his back, his legs in the air, while with his white paint brush he made slow circles in the sunlight. Did you ever see one of those beetles that get turned on their backs and can't get themselves right again? Like that.

But white instead of black. This struck Paulie as very funny, and he chuckled. A white beetle instead of a black beetle. He laughed out loud, showing his big white teeth.

Somebody would soon come along and help to put the painter right side up. First on the scene would likely be the Gorman woman. Pity he couldn't wait for that.

The forklift had never gone better; it paid to look after a machine.

The Long Consequences

Coming to sit in the boat had not been a good idea after all; the sun was too bright for reading. The wavelets trooping up the river made a spangle of golden points. She pulled on the mooring rope and, when the cot started to move, slow and heavy because the tide was running strongly now, she leaned back on the rope until prow bumped against granite. She gathered her books together where they lay scattered on the stern-seat, noticing how warm the planking was, and then stepped carefully onto the quay. The river came rolling to her from Curra Weir and beyond that from the city and the sea. The sedge leaned towards her too in that pleasant moving air, and the grey heron stood sentry among the grey stems, patience on one leg, Old Granny.

She turned away, and with her books under her arm went past the boathouse, feeling under her feet the springy turf that was made of so many years' wood-shavings. If you cut down through the layers you could count the years just like tree-rings, two hundred of them, each one thicker than the one before for the first hundred years, but after that thinning slowly until it would not be easy to find and number each layer, and then the final one, seventeen years before, the year she was born, the year after her father had closed the boatyard.

From the yard a stony lane ambled up the slope with many a stop and turn. Ferns grew damply in the moss on one side, and on the other the lichened stones gathered the sun's heat. The lane climbed a bit, then it checked again at the stony remains of a house. That was where Williams had lived, coachman at the Big House. If you looked and knew where to look you found the hearth and at one side a stone set at ground-level had a hole in it an inch deep, and that was where the fire-crane had swung. Ferns grew among the scattered rocks, their roots cool under the flags where once the fire had blazed. Further on a glistening stream crossed the lane and you could track that up the hillside to the coolest and greenest well. Her father often took a mug from the dresser and walked across the field to drink from it, even though the Lady's Well was much nearer.

At the highest point of the lane, Liz passed through the shadow of the square tower that people called Barrington's Castle. You could still reach the battlements by a winding stair in the thickness of the walls, and from the top you could look up the river or down, or across it to the hills. You could see also the double row of limes that pointed towards the Big House and even dimly among the trees make out the remains of what had once been the greatest house in this county and, for a short time, the greatest house in Ireland when Lord Ormsby had been Viceroy. The tower was a sad place now, jackdaws and bats its only inhabitants, cattle sheltering there from winter's wet and cold or from the flies in summertime.

Liz waited in the garden till she saw her mother come out the back door and go to one of the outhouses, then she went in quickly and took the key from the desk in the parlour. Her great-great-grandaunt Lettice looked down darkly and disapprovingly. Liz wrinkled her nose at her. Why should she disapprove?

Out then by the front door, pulling it quietly shut, across the lane and in by the tall iron gate to the churchyard. It was full of sunshine here, a sheltered place, and there was company that she was at ease with. She could tell where every grave was, almost what was chiselled on every stone. Here lies in hope of resurrection. The day Thou gavest, Lord. Happy are the dead. 1861 Elizabeth Wardell. James Nicolson. Hewetts, Greggs. Some day her own name would be cut on the limestone: Harriet Elizabeth Barrington. Just as well the other girls didn't know her first name. Old-fashioned, but she liked it because it was Family; there was another Harriet Gregg, alias Barrington, and a date that was either 1775 or 1795. Now this present Harriet, who departed this life in say, the year 2040 which would make her 77, and then she would lie here in the place she loved, with Hewetts and Pykes, Grahams and Greggs, Ibbotsons, Brownes and all her kinsfolk, with primroses.

Some people were afraid of churchyards. She had played here from her infancy, even though in those days the church had still been in occasional use. Then ten years ago the furniture and all of value had been taken away, to Achaveen. Graigue church, too, was no longer used, and the church in Ballykeeran had been demolished. The *other* graveyard, however, had lately been extended.

Or supposing she were to be buried in that other graveyard? Elizabeth O'Neill, née Barrington. RIP. Her loving husband, Thomas. Long rows of graves, all in line, no elms, no primroses. A tractor to cut the grass in summer instead of the gentle ministrations of old George Hillis. She stopped and stood quite still before the oak door, staring at but hardly seeing the black hinges and the peeling varnish. Tom was a nice fellow, and clever. What would everyone say? Her mother's disapproval was easily foreseen. Her father would kiss her. 'Whatever you think best, Elspeth,' (he was the only one who called her that), 'whatever you want, love. He's a nice lad,' always the generous word, and his eyes would smile, but he would be sad too, the last of the Barringtons and a tradition broken. The Canon would hardly be happy about it but he would, as usual, take no definite stand.

That would be left to Aunt Sarah. She would rage. 'Who is he? Tell me that,' and would her condemnation and bitter criticism be for his being Roman Catholic or for his lack of Family and Land? 'Why don't you find a nice Protestant boy?'

But whether Aunt Sarah knew it or not, time and history had taken away the nice Protestant boys and that was why Liz was going to the disco tonight with Tom O'Neill, and why she had decided, almost decided, to do nursing, to go away to Dublin to train, where perhaps there were such boys as Aunt Sarah imagined.

Then why had Frances Smith not found them? Trained in London, she had come back when she was quite old, well not old exactly, Liz's mother said she must be thirty-three at least, and married that dry old fellow of the Allens in Killin Grange. He must be well over forty, maybe he was fifty, he looked old and withered up. Of course he was one of *the* Allens and had several farms.

She fitted the huge key in its place and used both hands to turn it. The Allen stone was set in the wall near the altar, *sub umbra mensae* something, something, *sub umbra mensae in Lucem Vitae Eternae* something *Ricardus Allen, M.A. Hujus Ecclesiae diu Rector. Obiit* and the Roman numerals, she knew, meant 1798. There were other Allen names too in the corner near the main road.

The sunlight slanted in through the tall windows but she put her chair and desk in the shade, sat down and spread her books on the tiled floor. She took her history book and found 1798 and read a page or two but then shut it with a slap, because it seemed so unrelated to what she knew as history. No mention that in 1780 a Robert Barrington, with a younger brother, had set up a boat-building business near Curragh, that by 1800 he had twelve men full time in the yard, others cutting and drawing timber, that he owned or leased forests and mills, that half the cargo on the river was carried by Barringtons in barges they had built themselves. Salmon and eel-cots too. The family prospered in this new trade. But they turned their backs on the land. And new things came. In the twenties coaches, in the forties railways, and river transport failed to meet this competition. In 1889 when the Navigation closed down, boat-building was a declining trade. Fishing kept them afloat for a time, but their land in Dufferin and Cloonagloor had to be sold.

What was left? The too-big house, shadowed by the square

tower, twenty acres or so along the river set to Paddy Byrne, an abandoned boatyard. That was all. And the river, the river that had made the Barringtons and had destroyed them. The beautiful siren river.

Reading school history always brought her to this discontent, this feeling that history was here, in this churchyard, in the stones of the tower, in the springy turf of the boatyard, and to the feeling, instinctive, that the writer had somehow missed the point. She turned to an earlier chapter. '... Unpaid and potentially mutinous, the victorious troops were now, ironically, seen as a threat to the stability of the Commonwealth. A campaign in Ireland would keep them occupied, at a safe distance, and they could afterwards be paid with grants of land there.' How incomplete this version of it! The things that were not mentioned, the idealism, the passion for right and truth that had driven those plain people and that simple farmer to rise against and destroy the entrenched power of a tyrannous king and a corrupt system, and all those people ever since who had had the same quiet austere virtues, her grimly opulent great-great-grandaunt in her dark frame, and Grandfather, whom she vaguely remembered, and Robert her father, upright good people, and all the others around her sleeping now in the sunny silence.

Her father came in so quietly she did not hear him. He put his hands on her shoulders and kissed the top of her head. 'Stay a while?' She nodded. He put two cans of orange in the wall-niche. 'Would you like one now?'

'No, not now. Thanks for thinking of it.'

He sat on the altar step, took out his pipe, raising an eyebrow in question. 'Sure,' she said. He looked rested and well, as he always did on Saturdays; often when he came from work he looked haggard, and although he seldom spoke about the factory, she knew he was not happy there, a highly skilled man whose skill was no longer needed, working where skill was somehow distrusted. A gentleman ranker, the Canon called him. The Canon was an old snob but his comment was true in a way.

'How is the work going?' he asked presently.

She considered that. 'All right, I think.'

'What about maths?'

'If I get maths it will be thanks to Tom. He's able to make everything so clear. Trouble is I can't remember it afterwards.'

'Tom is a nice lad.' He lighted a match and applied it to his pipe, puffed, burnt his fingers and threw down the spent match among the others on the floor.

'Still quite determined to do nursing?' She nodded. They smiled at each other, understanding.

She must do something about that Geography Mr Bennet had given them. She took quick notes as she read. Her father smoked his pipe and the pleasant tobacco smell drifted past her. When he stood up and whispered, 'Bye,' she waved a hand and looked up briefly and smiled, and he slipped out as quietly as he had come.

Absorbed in her books, she was yet in a vague way aware of the stillness, aware of the shaft of dusty sunlight that now shone on her feet. I must bring a brush and a watering can and sweep the place, knowing she probably wouldn't now with the exam so close, but it would be nice to have it clean, and some flowers, the first roses were almost in bloom. She eventually pushed her books away and stretched herself. Mr Bennet had never been known to give a higher mark than C+, but he was a wizard tipster, always guessing shrewdly at what was likely to come up, so you felt pretty happy about Geography.

She stretched her arms above her head, then stood up and took one of the tins of orange and opened the door and stood looking out while she drank. She turned then and looked around her study, timber floor, one step up, tiles, four bright oblongs of sunlight bent across the floor and a little way up the far wall, her desk and chair, books scattered. It was a place not so big as to make you feel cold and alone, but big enough to walk around it if you wanted to think something out. Like who you were and where you were going and what you were going to spend your life at, and why you were determined to go away to Dublin when it might easily break your heart to leave this place, Harriet Elizabeth Barrington, almost seventeen. She pushed the door shut and went and looked in her mirror on the wall: fairly tall and a good figure like all the women in her family, dark heavy hair, nose a bit too narrow, but the eyes made you forget that, the eyes were the best part, grave, wide, steady. She took her hair and coiled it on top of her head. Then she opened her shirt and pulled it down, put her hands under her breasts, and looked very sternly at herself in the mirror. But no, she didn't look at all like her great-great-grandaunt Lettice, that mysterious lady. What on earth did they do to themselves to make them bulge up and out like that? Some kind of wire contraption? – she commenced to giggle. There came a knocking at the door and someone was calling 'Liz, it's me, Tom.' Hastily she fastened herself up again and went to let him in. He was standing at the bottom of the steps, smiling up at her. 'I met your dad and he told me where you were.' He looked around the little church. 'Say, this place is tops, isn't it Liz? Do you come here often?'

'Yes if the day is warm. But in cold weather, it would be too cold here. It is years since it was in use as a church.'

'Isn't it very small?'

'The congregation was probably never very big.'

'Who's that old fellow?' and he went to look at the Ormsby effigy and read Frederick Alnwick Ormsby, 4th Baronet, 1823. He read some of the other plaques. 'Are they related to you?'

'Some of them. Greggs mostly, Barringtons and Hewitts.'

'I suppose they all came over with Cromwell?'

'They did not,' she said defensively, and then was amused at herself. 'What does it matter who they came with or when? I'm here.'

'I'm glad you're here,' he said. It was not gallantry; he was too straightforward for that. They kissed, and she remembered how awkward he had been at first. He was six months older than she was. Only then did he notice and ask, 'What did you do to your hair?' but without answering his question she sat down at her desk and said, 'We'll go over that chapter Sister Pauline did on Thursday.' He sat on the floor and leaned his head against her knee.

When she stopped reading he said, 'History is bunk.'

'Not very original, Tom.'

'No,' he agreed, 'Henry Ford or somebody. Still, I could never get interested in history. Liz, is there anything to drink here? I'm parched.'

'There's a can of orange.'

While he drank he read the plaques near the altar. 'This one's in Latin … *Speravit vocati Ricardus Allen*, is he the same family as Dick Allen above? Rector? You wouldn't think Dick was related to a clergyman if you heard him the day he got caught in the cattle-crush between the two cows. MDCCXCVIII, when was that? You know, Liz, they say my family came from the north to fight Cromwell in – whenever it was – 1641.'

'Forty-nine,' she said. 'Do you believe they did?'

'Maybe. Why not?'

'Why don't you find out if it's true?'

'Yes, I suppose I ought to,' but she knew he wouldn't. He would spend his time fishing or swimming or hurling. Typical. Yet these were the people unconquerable who had applied that terrible patient persistent pressure, who had touched their caps and grovelled and had never forgotten.

'Anyway the two of us are on the same side now, aren't we?' he asked. He was such a simple fellow really, despite that quick brain, that you had to like him. He had the quality, too, of always thinking the generous thought, that reminded her of her father.

'Come on, we're here to do maths.' Maths they did for the next hour or so, but at the end of that time she was finding it difficult to concentrate. He realized this, looked at his watch and jumped to his feet. 'I must go home to my tea. I'll call for you about half past eight.' He went to the door. 'It's the last disco we'll be going to.' She looked up in sudden dismay and he hurried to explain. 'Until after the exam, I mean.' She stood up too and laid her hand on his arm and something was said though neither spoke. He put his arm around her, but she pushed him gently away and pushed him out of her little church. He pretended to stumble on the threshold, righted himself quickly, turned and kissed her again and then raced away to the gate, where he waved and said, 'Half eight. See you. Bye,' and left her smiling as she went in to gather her books. All the names looked down at her; the sun slanted in; if there were ghosts here they were happy ones.

She locked the door and turned her back to it and stood on the worn step where all the silent feet had trod. The grass had been trimmed and the place looked cared for; old George Hillis, only employee now of the Ormsby Estate, spent most of the fine days in summer here, a slow-moving presence, so unobtrusive that there were days when Liz had been here and when she returned home would have been unable to say with certainty whether he had been working there or not. He seemed almost part of the place. Its colours, its decorum, its silence, were his. He would sit on a stone and take his sickle in one hand, his whetstone in the other. The dexterity of his immense oaken hands fascinated Liz. With deliberate strokes he would bring the shining curve of steel to its perfection of concentration, a sliver that sliced thinly through juicy stems with minimum effort. Patiently, as though he had all time, he coaxed the bright arc to its keenest focus. He never appeared to hurry but had time to watch the sky and the brass weathervane, to tell her when the first swallows came or to lean across the wall and beckon to her because a peacock butterfly was basking in the autumn sun among grey stones. Yet the work was done, and done well.

Beside the path a heavy iron railing protected three headstones, three parallel graves, Abraham Barrington 1965, Daniel aged 72, Esther, John. 1880. The day Thou gavest. The oldest stone, near the wall of the cemetery, had 1766 on it; there was no earlier date. Where were the graves of the earlier members of the family? Probably in Achaveen, unmarked. Where was that first Sergeant of Dragoons who had come marching over the hill and into history?

The swing gate brought her out on the main road. A familiar car drawing a horsebox slowed and turned off along the Clover Ponds road, Egans going home from the gymkhana. Maura waved to her through the rear window. Old George was fond of saying that if you stayed long enough at Barrington's Cross you would see everyone in Ireland; he must have seen them twice over.

To her right the ground rose. There were the woods that surrounded the big house; beyond that was the higher land. Over that ridge they had come.

The horses stopped when they reached the top of the ridge. Did the riders involuntarily draw rein, as they almost certainly drew in a deep breath of admiration at what they saw. From the far western hills, woods and pastureland flanked the majestic river for many a mile, passed close in front of them, and faded in haze. The General looked sombrely into the east where lay the city he must take, and he looked also to the west where Carrickgriffon sat on its rock beside the river and shook behind its walls, the walls and rock and castle that he must have because they commanded the only bridge. The Colonel raised a hand, half turning in the saddle, and at once one of the horsemen that had come to a stop a short distance to the rear pushed his horse forward, his left hand gripping the reins while he leaned down with his right to unbuckle the holster and take out the heavy leather-and-brass covered glass which he passed to the Colonel. The Colonel grunted his thanks; Sergeant Barnton was a man who knew without being told; that was why he had been taken from the line. The General took the proffered glass and raised it to his eye, adjusting it delicately with his strong countryman's fingers. It was one of those soundless days that come in late autumn, colours muted by haze, no song of bird, and the silence was hardly broken, but rather accentuated by the clink of a shaken chain, the stamp of a hoof. Soon, however, the Colonel could hear the confused noise made by the main body of horse as they laboured up the hill behind them. He watched intently the heavy face of the General but could read nothing there. The glass in any case would show little more on a day like this than the naked eye could discern. He looked again along that leafy, watered valley and he allowed himself for a moment to dream: This is my last campaign. Soldiering is for young men. The General's voice broke in on his thought: 'It is a land worth fighting for.'

'Indeed yes,' he answered with enthusiasm. Those large heavy-lidded eyes were on him, eyes that saw too much, eyes grown sick with gazing on terrible things. 'We owe you much, Henry. Which will you have — to the left or to the right?'

'The right, if you will, General.'

The General snapped shut the glass and handed it to Ormsby. 'When Carrickgriffon is taken,' he said, and shook his rein.

'Thank you, sire. You are generous,' and the Colonel nudged his horse and the two men started down the slope.

She crossed the road to look at the Lady's Well; she knew George had been working at it. Dead leaves and duckweed banished, it was possible to see down to the grey sand-bed where the water pulsed upwards. But the roots of the tall tree that so long had sheltered the well had gripped and squeezed so that here and there the careful ashlar leaned out of line, and there was nothing George could do about that. The commemorative stone had suffered most. 'This well was cleaned and covered for the benefit of the people of Derryglass by Lady Winifred Ormsby in 1871.' A muscular root had flexed itself and pushed and split the stone in two; a thin green line of moss grew in the slanting crevice. And still the indifferent bubbles formed like magic among the pebbles and hurried to the top, just as they had done before ever Lady Winifred's improving eye had lighted on them. Would it sadden the Gracious Lady if she could know how little used or regarded her Good Works were now?

But a much more immediate question occupied Liz's thoughts as she walked home along the lane: what should she wear tonight to the Parochial Hall? She was tempted to wear a skirt and her black poloneck. She knew she would look well in it. But she was undecided; the other girls would probably be in jeans, and she didn't really want to be the odd one out.

Men of the World

Parochial House
Bawnarinka
12th April, '76

Mr WP Webster
c/o Severn and Dobson
The Book People
London

Dear Mr WP Webster

I was reading your book and I started to think about the church business, His Lordship will be sure to mention it again at Confirmation. No I can't find it, Ellie must have tidied it away, she's a terrible woman about tidying things but I mustn't say a word she's a good cook plain but good and that suits me because I like what I'm used to and I was brought up on plain cooking there was nothing fancy in that line in my young days. I hope you can read this, I mislaid my glasses looking for your book, it's Churches in Ireland since the Earliest Times or something like that. I have to hold the letter a long way from me or I can't read it I only hope you can. Now PJ, I think, has made a bit of a mess of that church of his but don't say that to him whatever you do. No, I can't manage I must go look for my glasses — that didn't take me long did it? they were on the hall-table, I should do what Ellie says and get a chain and put them around my neck. Now what does her note say? Ah yes she's gone over to Kelly's for a few eggs for the tea, will a poached egg be all right? Why wouldn't it it was alright yesterday, or was it scrambled? and when I want to say something to her I leave a note on the kitchen table. It is better than shouting at her, she's as deaf as a beetle but she won't let on. Where was I? oh yes — I only said to him it was a bit gaudy and he scowled and muttered, you know the way he goes on, but I'm used to him and anyway if a body can't offer a word of advice to his brother 'tis a queer thing, but you don't know him, of course you don't know me either and I don't know you but your book tells me you like churches and you like old churches to stay old the way they were meant. Now it occurred to me you're living in Ireland and not far away from me. I'd drive over myself only they've taken away my insurance. Sometimes I drive as far as the church sure it's only half a mile. He's unfortunate to have those nuns there anyway under his feet night and day and cooking for him, that Reverend Mother has him addled with her notions, side altars, petit foors did you ever hear anything like it? Plain cooking is what he was brought up on and far from petit foors. Ballymurphy in when 1906 was it? He's four years younger than I am. It was potatoes and butter, brown bread and home-made jam, and still we did alright, guinea-hen's eggs fried in butter not creamery butter either but real butter. Did you ever taste guinea-hen's eggs fried in butter? with some pepper. Or fresh trout. PJ and I used to tickle trout in Srool, and the mother would cook them over the open fire. Ah dear!

But never mind. Would you ever come over next weekend on Saturday or Sunday, or we could put you in Ellie's room, she wouldn't mind moving into the attic. You see I don't want the church changed but His Lordship keeps on – no don't come next weekend I've remembered we have Confirmation. I'll go and make sure. Yes I'm afraid Confirmation is next weekend. Now isn't it a wonder I'd forget it? but of course the young man is doing a lot of the work. I hope he doesn't forget anything His Lordship likes things to go smoothly, he's not bad as curates go nowadays, a lot of strange new ideas but fairly dependable. You couldn't possibly come over this coming week could you? I'm always here, so then I could tell His Lordship that I've consulted an architect – you are an architect? I'm sure you must be to know so much about churches and all those technical terms – clerestory, isn't that a fine word? – though I think you have Killeany spelt wrong and he wasn't Canon but Father Michael Molloy. I know this because he was a relation of my mother's who was a Hanrahan of Grangemore but sure you know that. Her grandmother was a widow woman when she married Peter Hanrahan and Father Michael was her second son by her first marriage. Tom the other son stayed in the home place and never married. He was the only PP of Leccan parish that wasn't made a Canon. He died sudden when he was only sixty at the races at Killone Park he died. The parishioners wanted Canon put on his tombstone for fear it would look bad beside all the other Canons if they didn't. They were fond of him you know although he was a cranky old – but I mustn't take up your time tracing old things, don't mind me correcting you, you're a young man. A lovely book, a lovely book, I got it from the library van they come around every month on the first Wednesday no the first no Wednesday it is, and if I think of it I go out to them. Tony kept it for me he thought I might like it and I did. There's Ellie coming in now, the whole house shakes when she shuts the front door but it would get His Lordship off my back ever since I came here it can't be that long could it? Well you can see His Lordship has of course PJ's church is very sound now and all that, but he used a lot of coloured paint and I don't like it. If you and I could just see that the roof is all right and do some little things like that. I'd like your opinion, it's asking a lot of you I know but I can see you are enthusiastic about churches. You know it's a Whesson church so it says on the corner and the date is on it too but I don't – could it be 1844? no it couldn't be as old as that and it was your book that answered a question. I often wondered why Whesson spent so much of his time designing churches in Ireland when he was a Welshman but you say he had a – well, well, human nature, you and I are men of the world, God works in strange ways, he often visited Ireland to see her. I suppose a man could design a church in atonement. Whesson designed a lot of churches in Ireland

I'm sure he's gone to heaven. What about a quick little visit
this week or a letter I haven't the telephone never got used
to them and not being very sharp of hearing and Ellie is as
deaf as a post but I mustn't complain there's many a priest
has no housekeeper. No don't ring the curate, leave him out
of this, he'd want a microphone, and come the weekend after
next I'll be expecting you. Come on Sunday it's a quiet day
once Mass is over. Last Mass is at eleven, you could go to that
and look at the church, but be in time or you'll have to stand
at the back and you won't see it properly under the gallery, and
come up to the house then and I'll be waiting for you. He
crows about it all the time you know, very hard to have to sit
and listen to him and he even got a booklet out and one line
in it about when it was built and who built it and *four pages*
about the re-decorating and who did that, and I still think
he made it far too bright and gaudy the way he went on and
on and His Lordship licking it all up and the rest of them
just sitting there and I knew Philly McCarthy was as smug as
anything because he has raised £25,000 to do his church and
his house and faith the house will be done first and poor Tom
Kelly looking as small as he could so His Lordship wouldn't
see him if he happened to look around. The whole roof will
have to be taken down they say. I'll talk to Ellie and we'll have
something nice for the dinner a nice bit of mutton and maybe
turnips and white sauce. What about – do you like a drop of
wine? that's quite all right, I don't object at all, in fact I used
sometimes have a glass myself at Lahinch, and there's always
a drop of Paddy here, very good if I get a cold, hot you know

with sugar and cloves. White, we'll have a white bottle and a red bottle. I'll talk to Ellie though I never cared much for the red now that's settled. Have I forgotten anything? Pity about the Confirmation really. You see I can tell by your book you're a man of taste and you won't make too many changes and I don't want the church changed at all but I told you that didn't I? and I must be brief and not take up your time. God bless you and send you safe here and safe home again. I'm looking forward to your visit.

Your old friend
James Fitzgerald PP

PS Or a duck would be nice wouldn't it. I'll talk to Ellie.

PS again maybe you're not, it's just occurred to me that you might already have been at church that Sunday? In that case come straight to my house and we'll look at the church later. It's really in very good shape except for that bit of a leak in the far corner and the floor boards near the font. Mrs Ronan put her foot through it she's an enormous big woman and Martin patched it up and it's a bit shabby I suppose. There's something wrong with the other wall too Martin says it's out of plumb but I wouldn't mind Martin he's not always seeing too well and it would be a good thing if we could get the heating working again before the winter. You haven't any idea what an architect would charge for that kind of job have you? there's that little job to be done in the sacristy too. I must give this to Ellie it's nearly post time. I didn't realize it was so late it's nearly ten to five.

Later. I was going to send you this at your book-people's address in London but I've changed my mind and I'll send it to your address in Ireland. I see you've written more books too good man keep at it. I've just found the book again it was on my desk all the time. You'd be a man knowledgeable about such things, — what — you wouldn't I suppose know what it would cost to get out a small booklet. Or come on Saturday and stay the night, with maybe a couple of pictures? I must close this, she's standing in the door with her hat and coat on and when that door is open there's a cold draught. I'll be expecting you. Stay two days till Monday I'd like that. We'll make a job of it and show them whatever Glenade can do Bawnarinka can do too and better maybe.

No we'll have a bit of bacon and cabbage Ellie says it's hard to get cabbage this time of year but maybe we'd manage, — the best dinner of all. We could have the dinner late if you'd sooner that, about seven I mean, I'll talk to Ellie — in haste, best wishes.

JF

A Wild Goose

I hate that Rosslare-Fishguard run. When the weather is rough it's a nightmare of sea and sick, and even at its best it's a miserable business. You leave Rosslare as day is falling and reach Fishguard in the thin dawn-time, the time when it's easiest to die, and you still have to face that long journey Clackety Clackety, Clack, Clackety Clack all the way across England and the south of Wales. There are two antidotes, sleeping and drinking. I've tried both and neither works.

In October the crowds are less. I found a quiet place to sit, comfortable enough, and thought I might sleep. I tried not to think of why I was going, time enough to worry about that when I reached London. So I lay back and closed my eyes, but that uneasy feeling wouldn't go away. They try to start the engines discreetly so that at first you don't notice but soon the whole world is throbbing to that dull pulse that beats against your brain and your stomach. I don't get sick, not physically, I just go crazy and can't stay still in one place.

In the bar I happened on a fellow called Connery from Clonmel. He played the tin whistle and we sang. There was also a North of Ireland fellow named Shaw and a young woman with him. Connery was young and worked in a hospital somewhere on the outskirts of London. He was full of fun and music and porter, and he was on his way back after a holiday at home and maybe the fun and music and porter were only to keep his heart up. 'Buachaill ón Éirne' was one of the songs.

Trouble and sorrow are brewing for me in the glen
More bitter by far than the black malt brewing of men
No shelter from pain but the leaf of the green bough above
And a twist in my heart is to see in the distance my love.

They have a pipers' club in Camden Town, I think he said Camden Town. He explained in earnest detail how to get to it; I'd be welcome there any time. Well, it's some place to go, when Cluain Gheal Meala is far away.

We were last to leave the bar. The boat had docked and then Connery couldn't find his luggage. He didn't look to me to be the kind of fellow would have luggage, but he had. We searched the whole place, deserted by this time, and there didn't seem much chance, but we found it, a hold-all kind of thing, biggish and awkward, with a zip and two handles on top. The zip was open, but this didn't seem to put him out at all, and when I picked the thing up, it clinked. He told me what was in it – large bottles – wrapped and not very well wrapped in old newspapers. And – I'm not making this up – spare ribs. God! Sad songs and large bottles and spare ribs – Ireland.

The Customs and Immigration men saw him coming and sort of shook their heads resignedly and he sailed through, but they stopped Shaw and the woman and took them away somewhere. It was October, no big crowds, and we found an empty carriage and spread ourselves and settled down with a bottle of stout apiece. I suppose if the spare ribs had been cooked we'd have started on them too.

Shaw found us. There had been some trouble, we never found out the full story except that she wasn't his wife but someone else's. After sampling the stout he went away again to find her and I suppose to make up whatever differences there were.

Then the ticket-collector called on us. Connery started searching for his ticket, found the large bottle was in his way, looked around for some place to put it and saw the ticket-collector's outstretched hand. The poor man must have been inexperienced; for the next fully three minutes Connery searched with great care through all his pockets, taking out the contents and examining them and putting them all back before moving on, while the ticket-collector fumed there like an eejit holding the large bottle in his hand. One up for Paddy and a victory over the might of the Empire exemplified in the ticket-collector with his natty uniform and his little neat moustache. Irrepressible humour, ineluctable melancholy. He found the ticket eventually, where he knew it was, in the first pocket.

Later, we each stretched out on a seat and went asleep, with our overcoats over us. I slept anyway, I'm not sure if Connery did. I woke up some time because I was cold, and he had the window open and his head out and was being sick.

We reached London at last. Peter was waiting for me, and I can tell you I was glad to see him and glad that he had a car to drive me to his place. Connery wanted to give me final directions for the Pipers' Club and he assured me over and over I'd be welcome but Peter had parked his car somewhere nearby and the parking time was nearly spent and so I had to say a hasty goodbye to Connery. The last I saw of him was there on the platform at Paddington, struggling with his luggage and with his legs, and trying to keep his coat shut against the cold. I should have offered him a lift but it was only afterwards I discovered his hospital was in the same direction I was going. He had lost his tin whistle and I never saw anyone look so bereft and forlorn. I could have asked, couldn't I?

Oriental Thomastown

In the stone and oak of Shee's Almshouse in Kilkenny city, an intriguing notice read: 'Imrat Khan, sitar, Barrie's Barn, tonight.' Somewhere near Thomastown, the word was, but where exactly no one knew.

The rain came down softly and incessantly, but we persevered. A potter in a castle gave us directions, put us on the right way, and soon we saw a pointing arrow. We followed many of these, pointing into the summer rain. A right turn, no road, just a narrow boreen that got narrower while the trees leaned in and dropped drumbeats of rain on the car-roof. Closed in tighter over the rutted lane – could we have read the sign wrongly? Would we be able to turn or reverse out?

We rolled at last into a great walled garden, wild and wet, but still minded, purple flowers drooping damply to the ground. At one side a complex of buildings, old, perhaps dwellings, perhaps once farm buildings. This was Barrie's Barn; we had reached the source of the Shee's Almshouse notice, island in the sodden fields. It *was* a barn, too, but more than a barn. High windows that began at the floor. At one end a cosy living-place, at the far end a huge hearth; the space between was for us.

Barrie was there, artist, owner of the barn. Present also, to present the musicians, was the remarkable Garech de Brún; he was, we were told, that most important person, the one who had caused it all to happen, and had brought the music-makers half-way across the world, on a magic carpet presumably.

Soon there came two Eastern gentlemen; they hid their hands in their robes and bowed, their brown eyes smiling, and then they squatted on cushions on a low dais just beside us near the great empty fireplace. To say that they made music doesn't adequately describe what they did. They took, one a sitar, one a set of little drums, or tabla, tuned and caressed them into life, made them laugh, made them cry, soar and sink and leap up again in torrents of music. For two hours, sitting at their bare feet, we lent them our ears, most willingly. There in that most unlikely place, with the damp fields all around us, and the trees, the East thrummed and sang, an exotic oasis, lost barn in a green world, while the Irish summer took its accustomed way and the monsoon rain gurgled in the gutters and spattered against the tall windows, perfect setting and accompaniment for a night that they filled for us with enchantment.

The Dunes

The sunlight gleamed silver on the sea, and on the long wet sands. The fishermen with their slanted fishing-poles stood patiently at the edge of the tide. Nearer, a great sea-beast lay on the machair; how lovely in the waves, but now …

A small wooden house stood near the dunes. On the veranda of the house a girl sat at an easel. When she became aware of me, she looked up — appraisal, acceptance, welcome. Her upper body, which I could see above the veranda-rail, was bare, though she showed no embarrassment nor even any conscious-ness that this might be thought unusual. And she smiled at me, a smile I had known always, perhaps from an earlier existence; it was the smile that men have known since mankind began.

When I went closer I saw that her painting was of sea and headland, of the fishermen on the distant invisible boundary between the tide and the shining sands.

'Is it difficult to get the colours right?'

She looked up quickly. 'Yes, that's just it. Some blue, a little green, a lot of grey. And yet it must glow with light. In my mind I see clearly the picture I want, but when I try to capture it, it escapes.' Then she asked: 'Did you see the dolphin?'

'Yes. How did it get in so far? Where was it going?'

'It was going to meet its destiny.'

Her answer startled me and I could think of no adequate response to it.

'This is a lonely place ... is it wise of you ...?'

The word seemed to surprise her. 'Lonely? I'm never lonely here. Besides,' she went on with apparent inconsequence, 'Gráinne will be here tomorrow. It's her house, you know.'

'But ... all alone? You don't know who I am.'

She looked at me, unsmiling now, gravely and steadily. She said, 'I am quite safe now that you are here. Quite safe. With you.'

If I had been startled before, this left me astonished and confused. No! not confused. It was quite clear; this was the girl I had always known I would find, and this day this place this meeting had all been fore-ordained.

She left her chair and leaned towards me, her smiling lips parted; I stood as high as I could, and with my hands on the veranda-rail I pulled myself up to reach her mouth.

It was not a passionate kiss. It was gentle, almost casual. It made no promises, it was not perhaps a prelude. It said nothing, yet I think now that it said everything. And from the instant when I had first seen her face, intent over the easel, I had known about this kiss.

'I was going to the dunes.'

'Wait for me,' she said. She took a dress and pulled it over her head, a simple dress, sleeveless, that concealed and showed all the soft curves. We walked side by side, her feet bare, mine sandalled. She took my hand. We crossed the patches of bare sand and the short seagrasses to where the dead dolphin lay, uncaring now of tide or wave, all its surging grace, its strength, its glorious joyous leaping beauty, all gone. She sighed and said, 'But what could it do? This is where it was meant to die.'

The dunes, from a distance so small, are huge slopes, mountains almost, of coarse loose sand that slips away from underfoot, great amphitheatres whose shifting walls rise up to the sky, their edges rimmed with stiff grasses; it is a place that shuts out the rest of the world and its clamour, shuts out even the sea, everything but the blue overhead. Sun-drenched hollows laced with wiry grass. No sound but the whispering of the wind, the very sound of silence. Shell-midden, spears of sea-holly, a grey feather that stirred in the faintest breath of air, a whitened bone. Desolate, and yet for us warm with joy.

We had arrived very late the previous night, after our long exhausting journey with just that one stop for a meal, and without even unpacking, had climbed into our narrow bunks and slept and slept. The first sunlight through the eastern window wakened me. She was still asleep, so I kissed her shoulder and went to the kitchen to make coffee. She came so silently that I heard nothing, and when I turned she was

standing naked in the doorway. Is she aware at all of the torrents that pour through me when I see her like that? Of the
tides of love and lust? That sinuous line from thigh to proud
breast, the perilous allure of beauty. She came to me and put
her sleepy mouth on mine. She was warm and heavy with
sleep. Then she pushed me gently away, picked up her mug of
steaming coffee from the table, and padded to the door, where
she turned to say, 'It will be warm and sheltered in the dunes,'
smiled and added, 'wait for me.'

I stood looking at the empty doorway, whence the light
had gone, the gleam and glow of her, the intensity, the radi-
ance. A woman's beauty is the scent of the rose, that entices
the predatory pollen-dusted bee.

Waiting on the veranda, I was struck by how little had
changed in the years since my first visit here. No fishermen
now, no dolphin, but the dunes seemed just as before; as for
the house, Gráinne's care had seen to it that all was secure,
minded, loved. Not painted of course, and no doubt more
grey and weathered, even more a part of this unchanging
place. The faded lettering near the door had not been renewed.
I thought I could make out 'r' and an elaborate capital, almost
certainly an 'S'. Sea-something? Spirit … Spindrift sounded
apt. Or Sanderling? Spirit of You set my spirit free. Eight
letters in all, maybe nine. I rather liked Sanderling. Sea
Breeze? It hardly mattered in any case; no postman, I was sure,
had ever been called upon to deliver a letter to that remote
place, and the naming of the house had been merely a whim
of the owner.

Already there was some warmth in the sun, but a breeze came from the far-off headland. Driven by that fresh breeze the tide would more swiftly flood the bay and the level sands would be pushed farther up the beach than last evening's tide; it would grope its way with slow deliberation towards the nearest slopes of the sandhills, the little lapping wavelets gulping greedily at mouthfuls of dry sand, remorseless, hasteless; it might even reach the grassy path from which I had seen for the first time this small house and the girl at her easel.

How many tides, since that first encounter? How many days and nights, each with its ebb and flow, unfailing, inexorable, the great bay emptying again and filling, under the changing moon? We had seen the same things that day, but each of us saw them differently: the shimmering sands, the far silhouettes of the fishermen, the silvered sea; the poor doomed sea-animal that had come on a brimming flood into this wide bay with its false promise of safety, to keep an imperative assignment; the things she had tried to put into her picture and that had eluded her.

She came and stood beside me. Now fresh as morning, no longer drowsy, she took my arm and placed it round her waist. She was wearing some flimsy blue thing, through which I could feel the softness of her body. We went down the three steps. Between the top step and the lowest she went from siren to concerned mother, and the serious face she turned to me made me say at once, 'There's no reason to worry. You know they love being with Gráinne. They think of her almost as a second mother. In any case, it's only three days. We'll see them again on Sunday.'

Reassured, she was happy again, and we began our walk, going first to where our dolphin had lain, because something of it might still be there. But no. Nothing. Only the short salt-bitten grass and the tiny flowers of heartsease.

'Nothing,' she said and tightened her arm around me as though that absence saddened her.

'If a storm brought it in, another could sweep away all trace of it.'

We turned away. 'Poor creature!' she said.

Reminded of storms, she told me about the wreck of the Sea Horse, of how, savaged by gales, the ship had been driven past the safe haven farther east, and been reduced to the forlorn hope of finding shelter here. But once inside those two head-lands, above the treacherous sands that no fluke could grip, and hunted down by a storm so venomous that it mocked at sea-anchors, the vessel was doomed. She foundered, and over three hundred men, women and children went down with her. 'A few were rescued, but three hundred or more were lost. And many of the bodies were never found. Some were washed up on the beach, and one, a child, was found here on the machair. The heart-break of it! The heart-break!' We were both silent then, thinking of that long-ago tragedy.

'And it's well known,' she told me, lowering her voice almost to a whisper, 'that on nights of storm you can still hear the phantom band of the Sea Horse here in the dunes. It was a troopship, you see, with its regimental band. Bridgit, the old woman who used to mind the bathing boxes, knew the air it plays. She called it *Ríl na Daibhche*, the Reel of the Dunes. But no one knows it now. Bridgit was a hundred years old when she died.'

'But,' I objected, 'who would be here in the dead of night in a storm? And if someone was here, he couldn't hear that Reel for the noise of the wind and the waves.'

'But there was an old house here long ago. Gráinne built her house on the foundations of the old one. That,' she explained with a wonderful lack of logic, 'is why she calls her house Sea Horse.'

We started then in the direction of the dunes, our dunes, arena born of conflict between wind and wave, a place of sand, grey marram, gull's cry, home of silence and mystery, keeper of secrets.

'The wind is cold,' she said, 'but we will find again that golden hollow. It has been waiting for us all this time.'

'Sometimes winds and storms bring changes. We might not ... ' but she turned, put her finger on my lips and said, 'Sssh! If not, we will find a better,' and asked me, the smiling lips and eyes confident of my reply, 'Glad of that day?' and I answered her in the words of the song, 'My life began again the day you took my hand.'

She leaned her head against my shoulder and sighed contentedly, and yet, as though she needed one further assurance, she said, and it was hardly a question, 'But what else could we have done? Was there a choice?'

Dawn on the Boyne
Brú na Bóinne

I meán-oirthear na tíre seo, tá mágh leathan féarmhar, idir an tSionainn agus Muir Meann. Is ins an dúthaigh sin a lonnaigh treabh de na feirmeoirí ba thúisce tháinig go hÉirinn.

Gluaiseann abha go mall maordha tríd an machaire, agus ó ba léir dóibh gurb í an abha sin agus a fo-aibhne, le comhoibriú Lúgha, dia na gréine, a bhronn saibhreas ar an gceanntar, thugadar Abha na Bóinne mar ainm uirthi mar omós do Bhóinn, bandia na féile, na feise agus na torthúlachta.

Thagaidís le chéile i gcomhthionól, rí agus mór-uaisle uile na treibhe mar aon le saoithe is baird, aos dána agus aos éigse, ar bhruacha na Bóinne ar uairibh áirithe sa bhliain chun na déithe a onóradh d'réir mar tuigeadh san dóibh: an grian-dia, Lúgh a d'fhéach anuas orthu ón spéir agus a thug teas agus samhradh; déithe na báistí is na gaoithe; dia dorcha na hithreach, agus Bóinn féin, chun buíochas a ghabháil leo agus chun meas agus tairbhe agus rath a iarraidh.

Five thousand years ago, before ever a Pharaoh thought of building a pyramid, a group of farming people left Brittany by sea in search of a new home. They skirted Cornwall and the Scillies, and leaving Wales on their right hand they continued their voyage, north and north again, following Ireland's eastern coastline to their final landfall, a seaboard nameless then, that in the centuries that followed has had many names and that we now call county Meath. They found a great wide plain where grass grew in abundance and it was there that those early farmers decided to settle. Settled, and in course of time, prospered and multiplied.

A river flows serenely through that chosen land, and since they believed that it was the river that gave the plain its richness, they called it the River of Bóinn, in reverence to Bóinn, the she-god of welcome, intimate embrace and fertility. It is known now as the Boyne.

This river was their life. From its faraway sources it brought water sufficient for all their needs. It was their highway, from its small beginnings far inland to its wide estuary on the sea. It fed them: they had a harvest from the land; a second harvest when the salmon returned to the water that they knew as home; and that same river filled and enriched the sea, from which they took their third harvest.

It was tribal belief that the high goddess had at all times looked favourably on them, even from the beginning. They knew she had helped them to find this happy place; the wide sea-mouth had beckoned, the tide was surging in, and they rode that rising tide as far up the river-valley as it could carry them, then hauled their ships ashore, knowing at once that they had reached their destination, their destined home. They were aware of a debt of gratitude for her guidance and benevolence.

At the ordained times they came together on the banks of their river, king and princes, chieftains, captains, bards and druids, learned men, followers of the noble trades, poets and music-makers, and the smaller people also, with the purpose of paying homage and honour to the gods, as they understood those to be: Lúgh, chief of the gods, who looked down from the sky and gave them summer and warmth; and also Bóinn and the gods of rain and wind, and the dark earth god, to give thanks and to beg for their favour and protection, for bountiful harvest and prosperity.

At a point on the northern bank where the river bends south towards the sun, there is a low hill which gives a view to the four quarters over the level lands, a fit place they thought for a memorial cairn. They wished to repay their debt.

They met in council; they debated; they came to agreement. The project they approved was epic and would require all the energy, skill and strength of every member of the tribe, all their art and science, their utmost ingenuity and dexterity. It would be a challenge and a test, and in order that there be no error, every aspect of the work must be tried and verified beforehand. It was intended as the highest expression of their determination, of their construction genius, and not least, of their intellect and subtle art.

On that small hill they gathered on the appointed day. Those highest in rank in their coloured robes, watched by the others, the humble ones in grey. The sun shone, and this was taken as a sign of approval from Lúgh. He was the one they feared, the only one who showed himself to men, fearless, indifferent. Bóinn they loved, mother of creation and abundance; Lúgh they feared.

A tall narrow stone had been set firmly upright on the level top of the hill. Then as the druids chanted, the king was presented with the ceremonial spear; he walked with deliberate steps to where the shadow of the stone lay on the ground, raised the spear and held it for a moment poised above his head, then brought it down on the end of the shadow, and the throng gave three great shouts.

When a fence had been constructed around that bend of the Boyne, none were allowed inside but those of high rank, the learned ones, and those whose labour or skill or building craft was needed. At first their work centred on the tall pillar-stone and its shadow. Men whose study was the heavens and their changes, moon and stars, now turned their minds more particularly to the movement of the sun as shown by the shadow's movements, and if any one of these astronomers felt vaguely uneasy (because this was Lúgh, the sun-god, whom they dared not look at), none spoke of his misgiving since the work had been agreed by all the tribe. They marked and recorded at every noon when sunlight threw a shadow. Until the summer solstice that shadow shortened; by slow degrees from that time on it grew in length. What was new in this was the exact recording of their knowledge. Those who directed and recorded were men who had learned many many things, yet were not satisfied, but wanted to know more. They lusted after knowledge of all kinds, of the heavens, of the gods, of man and his place on the earth, of life and death, good and evil, and yet seemed unaware, or indifferent, that that insatiable curiosity does not make men happy but that great sorrows brood there. Whatever fears they may have had, however, were set aside; they continued their research and when they were certain that they knew all they needed about the winter sun's movement, and not until then, the building of the great Brú began.

Twenty years of their lives they gave to its building, years of unremitting labour. More than a thousand workmen, women too and children, each in accordance with ability, all helped. And not a few who toiled hard and willingly and had seen its simple beginning died without seeing the final achievement. Hundreds of thousands of tons of stone, timber, sand and earth went into the making of this vast dwelling for the goddess. The world's biggest house, Brú na Bóinne, a circular mound ninety paces across from side to side and covering an acre of ground. Ten spear-lengths in height. Quartz and granite had to be shipped from the Wicklows and the Mournes, though most of the rock was quarried nearby, and thousands, many thousands of water-rolled stones were taken from the river, just half a mile away. The sacred stones were chosen by their king, advised by those who had experience of the many different rocks; then the most gifted masons exercised their cunning to produce works of beauty.

And beneath this marvellous cairn was a greater marvel; on the south-eastern side was the high luminous doorway, with its slit-window above, then a passage leading for five and twenty paces between rows of tall boulders to a chamber at the heart of the Brú, where the stoneworkers had applied their rich lithic art to the walls and the great stone basin. This was the sanctuary of the goddess Bóinn, adorned with every bright wonder.

The last carpet of fine sand was laid on the floor of the sanctuary in autumn of the final year. Should the massive door be rolled shut for security, or left open in welcome? Open, they decided, though no doubt if the goddess wished to come or go a closed door would be no deterrent. They prepared for winter; when crops had been harvested and the days began to shorten, they must often have gazed proudly at the green mound with its stone girdle that stood looking down on the river, a mound that twenty years before had not existed, the triumphal work of their hands. What surprise if they were proud! Pride, mixed perhaps with some anxiety: the shortest day would soon come, a time of the greatest importance. That day when the pulse of life beats slowest almost to a stop was, they believed, the occasion of Lúgh and Bóinn's assignation when the two met in joyous embrace, and the generous she-god shared her new fertility with all, with men and women, river and plain, herd and harvest. That was their hope, for despite all their previous experience they still feared the wolves of winter. They feared the dying of the light and what even greater terrors it might forebode.

They gathered long before sunrise. Ten had been chosen, those of highest honour, who walked in silence one by one through the high doorway and along the narrow passage into the central room. The faint light of a torch threw dancing shadows on the walls, on the roof-corbels, on the granite basin newly filled with water from the river. Outside were grouped those next in importance, among them the astronomers and the directors of the vast undertaking, and by little and little further and further away, the others, until at a distance was the most numerous group, the labourers, the unconsidered, who gazed upward in wonder, patiently or impatiently, with curiosity, with apprehension, perhaps without understanding clearly what to expect. The night was cold; the minutes crept by; chanting could be heard from the hill; then the black silence fell again.

What were their thoughts, those grey unconsidered? Did they wonder if the huge house that had cost them so much in toil, in injuries and deaths, would make any change in their lives? The open door was meant for Bóinn, but suppose Lúgh entered? And stayed? Suppose he became trapped there, what would that mean? Would it mean that the days, instead of lengthening would get shorter and shorter until – dreadful thought! – no, it was not good to think in that way. Everything would be well, they must trust their leaders. And yet ... They had come, indeed, though they hardly knew it, to the dark unspoken thought, too terrifying to be put in words, that lay behind their mid-winter ceremonies.

It was otherwise with those grouped near the high entrance, whose knowledge and search for knowledge had driven this huge project, who had had a high ambition and seen it carried to completion. The dawn came, and by that timid grey light they saw a clear sky and were elated. Impatiently they awaited the sunrise and when the first bright ray appeared above the horizon, they watched intently. The sun-god leaped boldly up. There was nothing of diffidence or humility in him, yet they must wait until the full circle of brilliance had lifted itself free of the earth before they heard the druids' secret song. Then they knew with certainty that all was well, was as they had foretold, that a seal had been put on their endeavours, and they were exultant. Fame and reward would be theirs.

But what of the ten in the central chamber? It was they who saw the marvel most clearly. They saw the powerful pulse of light that entered by the narrow opening in the lintel and penetrated to the very centre of the Brú, bestowing on the goddess the gift of new life, which she in turn would pass on to the water of the river and the soil of the great grassy plain. At once without pre-meditation they shouted ... a shout that stopped again as quickly, as though they realized that noise of any kind was unbecoming. Silence fell. Yes, they knew that success had crowned all they had toiled for. A palace for Bóinn, yes, but did even one or two among them consider something else: that maybe they had gone too far? For the first time human eyes had seen this intercourse of the gods, and would it have been more seemly if it had not been wit-nessed? It might have been the wish of Bóinn and of Lúgh that their coming together should take place in secret as it had done since the beginning of the world. It had not been their purpose to offend the gods, rather the opposite, but was that the result of all their mighty exertions? They stared at the golden shaft that ran straight from Lúgh through the crevice above the door. It fell in a yellow pool on the sanded floor and the granite basin; it fell on the feet of the occupants, some of whom moved aside as though unhappy at having that bright light shine on them. And they were silent. From outside they heard the *sanas-laoi*, the druids' mystic chant, but in the chamber there was an uneasy silence.

The days went on, however, and everything seemed as before. Even though in some minds there were small doubts lurking vaguely on the edge of consciousness, those who had worried were calmed as time went by with no sign of change. What should they fear? That they might have roused the anger of the vengeful Lúgh, or that they might have hurt, without meaning to, the gentle goddess who had always shown them warm regard and goodwill? But the spring days lengthened as they had always done, the sun still shone and grasses grew, and the seasons followed one another in their turn. Sun, cloud, wind and rain came in due course. And the river continued to bring out of the south its burden of life-giving water, still flooded the inches in winter with fertile silt, and no-one saw any lessening of Bóinn's beauty and bounty. Trout and salmon leaped in plenty; insects buzzed in the drowsy summer heat where their cattle stood knee-deep in the shadowed water. Willow and alder, the little gilded fly and the stealthy otter, run ripple and reach. The slow laden craft that swung heavily to the current, the dancing coracle light as a hazel-shell on the brimming water. Swallows swooped to drink on the wing, under dark woods or in glittering sparkles of sunlight, where the silent swans sailed by and the grazing cattle never lifted their heads. The grey heron that fished the shallows, and the sudden flash of blue that said kingfisher. Still pools and gliding pebbly bars, ford and white weir. The shouts and splashing of children at the swimming-stone. And there were also the noisy winter geese that came from no-where, that spoiled the river pastures so that their animals would not graze there, but that stayed only a short time; as soon as days grew long they spread their grey wings and followed the tides northwards, back again to the mysterious land from which they had come.

71

This is the river and these are its gifts, gifts of the she-god — water-lily, dragonfly and blue salmon, pulsing current of life. These remained unchanged; and Bóinn's high cairn also, on its eminence above the valley, became, with time, an accepted and reassuring presence, a reminder of the magnificent self-belief that had enabled them to plan the masterpiece and bring it to triumphant reality, a reminder of that time of exuberant creativity based on a powerful direct certainty and a shining courage. It was the same courage and daring that had brought them to this green land of promise, braving the long sea-lanes and the anger of the storm. Built as a tribute to their benefactress and as a worthy tomb for their kings, Brú na Bóinne stood proudly also as a tribute to their own enterprise and resolve. It is a wonder and a mystery, older than the pyramids of Egypt, fitting monument to a great race of whom little is known, whose only building-tools were of stone or wood and the strength of their limbs. They are a people lost in the dim forgotten years; if they seem to speak still through the Boyne tombs and especially through Bóinn's regal house, the whisper that comes over that vast emptiness says little more than, 'See what we have built.'

The proud cairn guards its secrets, brooding over the bend of the Boyne. It has known great change, all the many changes that the turbulent centuries have brought, but still the tides fill and ebb in storm or calm and grasses grow, the river still sparkles in the sun and larks are singing above the peaceful fields. These things remain, and the kings asleep in the ground.

Colkitto's Tooth

Our history teacher in Avondhu, Mr Cronin, was a man before his time, in having a wide and generous view of what constituted history. With willing help from his friend Mr Nyhan, the undertaker in Mallow, who owned a big black car, we went on fine Saturdays (provided there was no funeral on that day) to various places of interest in or near the town: the site of an ambush, or a dolmen or ring fort, the spa on the edge of town, a ruined abbey or castle, the point on the Blackwater where O'Sullivan Beara forded the river on his epic retreat – any one or more of these might be included, and he could bring together in a short time a great variety of sometimes unexpected characters, such as Fionn mac Cumhaill, the poet Spenser, Tom Barry, Canon Sheehan and the Man from God knows where, whose name I think was Thomas Russell and who came from Mallow, according to Mr Cronin. So God wasn't the only one who knew. All of them were history, because as our historian explained, 'They're all in the past tense.' Even the railway station and the sugar factory were not ruled out, though he might have found it difficult to explain their tense, as both were still in operation. The historical present, maybe.

At one Thursday class he announced, 'Saturday afternoon we go to the site of one of the most important battles to take place in Ireland. I don't want volunteers; I want enthusiastic volunteers.' As most of the students would be playing football on Saturday, the number of volunteers was seldom more than six.

We discussed after class what battle it might be. There seemed little choice. Limerick? But that was a siege rather than a battle. Ballyneety? No, a minor skirmish. And Kinsale was thirty or more miles away, out of our range. We were surprised then when, on the day, we headed a few miles northwest to Kanturk, and on our way there Mr Cronin told us that our destination was Cnoc na nOs. None of us had ever heard of it. He insisted, however, that it was a key battle, even if seldom mentioned in history books, important for the numbers engaged, for the numbers killed and especially for its critical effect on the struggle between the English parliament and King Charles, a struggle which of course involved Ireland too.

We stopped at the hill that gives its name to the battle and he gave us some details of it: the English army under Lord Inchiquin was only a little over half the strength of the Confederates whose commander was Lord Taafe. Taafe's second-in-command was the redoubtable Alexander Mac Donald, Alastair to the Scots, and known to the English as Colkitto (a corruption of Mac Cholla Chiotaigh) who led a thousand Mac Donalds of Islay, Kintyre and Antrim, with other clansmen from Keppoch, Atholl and Badenoch. He and his men had fought all through the Scottish campaigns under James Graham, Earl of Montrose, the Royalist general. Montrose's great gifts as a commander and the fierce courage of the battle-hardened Highlanders had brought victory after victory, including Inverlochy, a triumph of strategy, where 1700 Campbells were killed, and the power of that great clan broken, and also Auldearn, where Alastair so distinguished himself that he was knighted on the battlefield by his commander. Montrose, brilliant strategist and tactician, defeated every Parliamentary army sent against him, and in all those battles the presence of Colkitto and his men was decisive. When it seemed safe to do so, he left with half his Highlanders to attend to some private Mac Donald business in the west, leaving the remainder under the command of his Irish Lieutenant, Maghnus Ó Catháin, and it was while Colkitto was away that Montrose was surprised and defeated at Philiphaugh.

After the royalist cause had been lost in Scotland, Alastair and his mercenaries came to Ireland to fight with the Confederates against the Parliamentary forces. To both the Scots and the Irish he had become a hero, another Cúchulainn whose very appearance and legendary fighting qualities were worth a thousand men and whose fame outshone even that of the great Montrose. Tradition makes him eight feet tall, which may be an exaggeration, but big he was and powerful; such a man wielding a claymore would be a dangerous enemy for anyone to face, but the fact that he was left-handed, *ciotach*, made him doubly difficult to deal with.

At Cnoc na nOs, Alastair commanded the right wing of the Irish army, and when battle was joined he and his Highlanders charged the English immediately in front of them and drove them back in disarray. The very success of that charge may have contributed to what followed. Both Inchiquin and Taafe must have seen the danger to the exposed right flank of the Confederate army, but the able and experienced Inchiquin was first to react; he sent his cavalry around to take the Irish in flank and rear, they gained the crest of the hill, Taafe's line broke and fled, and the day was lost. It became a massacre.

The memory of the thousands left dead or dying on the slopes of Cnoc na nOs remained for long a bitter wound in the hearts of the people and became the subject of many songs of sorrow and lament. For the Confederate cause it was disastrous.

The battle-site on the day we visited was calm and sunlit, a green hill where shadows drifted, sheep and their lambs in the fields, a hawk hovering above. Afterwards we were brought to see a monument where there was a great mound of bones, the remains of Taafe's army of Irish and of Alastair's 'redshanks'. The bones were contained within a structure of cut stone and iron bars; it was possible to reach in between the bars and touch the skulls, which I did. I did more – I prised a canine tooth from its socket (young fellows of fifteen are generally not squeamish in such matters). I kept it in my pocket and liked to pretend it was Colkitto's tooth, that fearsome warrior who had faced and vanquished a thousand enemies, and whom I imagined towering, kilted, bearded, his *claidheamh mór* in his huge left hand, his open mouth yelling a defiant battle-cry through his gapped teeth.

Since my first visit, I have learned more about that battle in 1647. Mr Cronin's opinion of its importance was difficult to deny; after that sad day, Taafe's great army of perhaps 8,500 men was no more, and that loss may have meant the difference between victory and defeat for the Confederates in Ireland, and who knows, for the royalist cause in England too.

As to that eye-tooth, the chance of its being Alastair's was always remote, since thousands fell that day. But I was a slow learner, or maybe I just wanted to ignore the facts. My faith in my talisman weakened, however, when I learned later that Alastair had not been killed in the fighting, but had been forced to surrender and had been put to death afterwards by order of Inchiquin, in contravention of accepted rules of war. And when one day I discovered that the tooth was missing from my pocket, I felt no regret; by that time I knew that shortly after his death, Colkitto's body had been carried to the quiet cemetery at Clonmeen and buried with dignity, and there he sleeps, far from the noise of battle and the scenes of his triumphs, in a peaceful place where few remember even his name.

Gallia Est

My heart is in Ireland and yet sometimes it longs for the lovely land of France. There, it seems to me, is a happy fusion of old and new, with an assured sense of permanence and stability under that ripening sun. It is fruit and food and an old unique culture.

We may walk a bright busy street which might be in a modern town or city anywhere, except for language and other small differences that we become aware of gradually and that make for a certain style which the French seem able to achieve effortlessly and instinctively. Turn into a narrow, shadowed side-street. An arched doorway, and we are in an ancient church, dim but not gloomy. It is minded, flowered, a pleasant place. A brass tells us it was built for his peasants by a great local landowner, an aristocrat, long swept away in bloody revolution. A good man, in his way, with thought for his people, though we may surmise that it was his people who really paid. Well, so did he, ultimately. The brass speaks in French only. But of course, why should it be otherwise? They are confident in being themselves, in being different.

The street dips towards the river and now under our feet there are huge stone blocks, and we are brought to a stop by seeing at a street-corner the ruts made by Roman chariot-wheels. The building at the corner is made in its lower courses of the same massive shaped stones. We can put a hand on the stone and turn to each other and gossip, just as Roman citizens or soldiers did two thousand years ago. Careful of our toes, of course. We might discuss why they built so heavily, so practically, so grimly, with, it would seem, no ambition towards beauty; and yet in this same great country of so much variety and contrast, I have seen against the sky a thing of air that they created, of arch above arch above arch, built by an inspired plumber, functional indeed, and yet one of the most beautiful buildings I have ever seen.

Peaceful now, this land was not always so. Wars big and small, local or larger, have seldom ceased here, Visigoth, Frank and Hun, Huguenot and Cathar, Plantagenet and Sansculotte, Viking and Gauleiter. The last half-century has been the longest continuous peace they have known.

In a small sanded place with a tree or two for shade, a seat or two, they are playing a game of boules. I know nothing of the game – perhaps they were playing it before the Roman legions marched in through Provence – but I can watch it happily, if not in the flesh, at least in the mind's eye. I see a black beret snatched off by its wearer and thrown on the ground, but that is the nearest thing to violence. A little money may change hands, no more, I hope, than the price of a glass of wine. Long may they continue to play this, when the other games of the world have been invaded, corrupted and destroyed by money.

James Elroy Flecker, a lover of things Eastern, loved France too. It was he who wrote, 'I will go to France again and tramp the valley through.' Nowhere is it more rewarding to tramp the valley through. The vines climb up the hillsides, row on row, vineyard on purple vineyard. They know how to live; they grow wheat and they make bread; they grow the grape. Who else know the grape as they do? Wine-making they learned from the Romans, who learned it from the Etruscans, and that was more than two millenniums ago, however you count it. Newcomers may make good wine and make money by it, but the lore and the love, how could they know that?

The vast forests, oak, pine, walnut, beech and sweet chestnut, with a glittering, sugared Alp showing beyond. Those magnificent rivers. The fields of grain, of fruit, of sunflower and lavender, in the perfumed sunshine. A fertile soil, tended and nurtured, loved and sometimes perhaps hated, by a resilient people, with a skill, care and passion that has outlasted the centuries, that has taken thousands of years of sustenance from the land and left it no poorer.

Tower on its sea-rock, guarded by the crawling tide. Château brooding on ancient glory. Nearer, more intimate things: shuttered noontime windows, café tables, sun-dappled.

Every inch of this country – should that be every centimetre? – is steeped in history, a history that flames in pageantry, in great names: Burgundy, Lorraine, Normandy, Aquitaine; Valois, Guise, Angevin, Bourbon. Names that are more than names because of their associations: Avignon, Chartres, Giverny, Languedoc, Somme, Orleans. Cities whose stories go back into mists beyond our seeing. Monarchs and dynasties. Heroes – and villains. Roland, Charlemagne, Napoleon. Epic triumphs and defeats. Poitiers, Azincourt, Waterloo, Moscow, Sedan and Austerlitz; far echoes of the barricades and fainter whispers of Roncesvalles.

Gallantry and infamy, halls hung with the banners of king and emperor, 'their chariots, purples and splendours'. But now the many dukedoms, counties and viscounties, kingdoms and principalities that have gone to the making of this republic, having put their rivalries and hostilities aside, stand together at last to form that strong bastion of Europe, *entre deux mers*, centred on the luminous island on the Seine that shares its name with France.

And still I haven't mentioned her thinkers and her artists: the troubadours, singers, poets and composers of music; her artisans and craftsmen in stone or clay or fabric; or those whose awareness of line and colour and creative response to that awareness, the beginnings of which are buried in caverns of time before history began, have made Paris pre-eminent and filled the galleries of the world with French art.

It is true that France, more perhaps than any other country, depends on nuclear energy. True also that France has a heavy share of responsibility for the wars that for centuries have torn Europe asunder, as also for an ignoble part in conquest and colonization, and that many of its citizens look across the Mediterranean towards Africa with feelings of regret, or of anger, or it may be, of guilt. The creaking of the tumbrils on the blood-spattered cobbles may still come faintly above the roar of Parisian traffic, or so I imagine, and sadly I know too that France is one among those former imperialists that by their armaments stimulate and maintain wars all over the world. Yes, I know some of the faults, but perhaps at this remove I may be allowed to ignore them, to see the bright colours and forget the shadows.

Ebbed Seas

There was a girl in Umbria whose name was Inachis, meaning Butterfly in some language or other, so she told me. Sanskrit, maybe. I explained to her that I wanted to get to Greece. Surely it ought to be possible to get a place as a helper on an archaeological dig in Greece? If perhaps she knew any archaeologists …? She said plaintively, 'I thought it was for myself alone that you …?'

'It was, it is,' I assured her, 'but I love Greece too.'

'You know Hellas of course?' she asked me. 'Andreas Hellas?'

'Of course,' I said. I found out afterwards that he was *the* man, professor of classical archaeology in Athens. Or Cairo? I'm not sure if that was his correct name, but something like that.

'You are a millionaire?' she pressed.

'Yes.'

'Then there is no problem.'

When these details had been seen to, we set out and reached Euthalia, which is a tiny village on a sheltered bay, three sardine

boats, but there had been a city there once, a thriving Greek
city of a thousand souls.

We had been there only a short time when Inachis took me
aside and spoke very seriously. It had begun to strike her that
archaeology was not as glamorous as she had hoped, that archaeologists were expected to get down on their knees and actually get
their hands dirty. So she spread her dainty wings and departed
to more civilized places and pursuits, leaving me broken-hearted.
To my surprise, however, my heart mended within a day or two,
with considerable help from Peacock. Peacock was an interesting
girl, silent for the most part, but able to say plenty with her dark
lustrous eyes; when she did speak, it was in a wonderful mixture
of demotic Greek (very demotic), what I took to be Persian,
and her weird version of New York slang.

When last year I visited Euthalia again, a sentimental journey,
I found that one of her phrases was still used by the citizens in
times of stress, though none of them seemed to be clear about
its meaning, they just liked the sound of it – '*Chiffeta astoni*.'
They certainly didn't know they were quoting Peacock. I was
pretty sure I knew the meaning, but I wanted the local opinion.
The innkeeper when questioned remembered the diggers, but
could throw no light on the origin or meaning of the words.
'Ask the harbour-master,' he advised, 'he knows everything.'

The harbour-master put on his peaked cap and a face of
great seriousness, as befitted his office and reputation. He said,
yes, it might have originated with 'the diggers'. 'It's Italian, of
course, and has something to do with melons. I am sorry I
cannot be of more help – I have matters to attend to.'

To return, however, to my first visit to Euthalia: our director was a Cretan who smoked aromatic Egyptian tobacco in a curvy pipe that complemented the curves of his magnificent moustache. He had been a builder of pyramids, I feel sure, but had come down in the world. No whip now, and instead of Hebrew slaves he had a motley gang that included two boisterous young Italians, both called Tony, which could be confusing at times; a rather surly Bulgarian; three or four Greek girls from the university – Melissa, Penelope, Sybil, names like that; the dark, warm girl whose name was Peacock and who may have been Persian; a young lad from the village and two older men who were employed to do the heavier work. There was also one other, from the outer parts of the world, from 'where the Atlantic raves outside the western straits'; I felt very much the outlander, but they accepted me, and from them I learned a lot of useful everyday Greek, which was of course the language of the group. I tried my lame Italian on them once, but the two Italian boys hooted with laughter, while the others kept a polite silence. I used English; they shook their heads; I thought I heard the word Byron but it may have been some other word. Then I spoke to them in Irish. They smiled; for one throb of the artery I wondered if some old, old memory had stirred in their collective subconscious, some race-memory from thousands of years past. But no, I could see by their faces that it was all Greek to them.

We trowelled through earth and shards and history, and because our Cretan had mellowed with the years (there were flecks of grey in his moustache), we stopped often to drink from the well, to look out across the blue to where my drowsy ship rode at anchor near the cape, or to swim in the wine-dark sea.

Evenings, from the western rocks, we watched suns sizzle down into the Mediterranean; we drank the tarry wine; someone played lonesome things on a pipe. We laughed a great deal, and sang, and our Cretan was suspicious of us, though of what exactly he suspected us I don't know. Perhaps of being young and happy. It was a golden time, every day the sun shone without fail from a clear sky, I was nineteen years of age, and everything was possible.

Rich

He drifted into the yard, where Mam was feeding the hens, and asked for a bit of bread, 'a stale bit will do, ma'am, and maybe a small drop of milk, and God bless you.' Mam sized him up with one shrewd glance and said, 'Go up there and sit on the chair by the kitchen door. I'll talk to you in a minute.' Then she looked around for me. I had slipped into the stable to avoid being given a job to do, even though I was curious about the stranger and wanted to know what was going to happen. But of course Mam knew where I was, Mam knew everything. 'Tom, come out here and look after the hens,' and then headed for her kitchen. The teapot sizzled as usual at the edge of the fire, so our travelling man got a mug of scalding hot tea with plenty of sugar and milk, and both brown bread and white soda with currants in it, and plenty of butter. 'He looks hungry,' Mam said to Aunt Kate and it was Aunt Kate who did the catering while Mam went to talk to him. I heard her asking about his family but he didn't make her any the wiser.

He was vague about his name – as indeed about most things, especially anything to do with himself – and somehow he finally became known as Rich. Where had he come from? Why? What had he worked at? Had he a wife, a family? We found few answers to these natural questions. The one thing that was not vague about him, as we soon learned, was his love and knowledge of horses, and so it seemed most appropriate that he eventually wound up sleeping in the loft above the stable, where a straw mattress and the proximity of the two big plough-horses helped to provide him with some small comfort.

Naturally, Daddy had to be consulted about this when he came back from the fields. What was to be done about the newcomer? I suppose I knew even then, the way children know such things without being told, that the matter had already been decided, but Daddy had to be asked for his opinion; the conventions had to be observed.

The wanderer showed no inclination to leave, but behaved, with a gentle insistence, as though he thought this was where he was destined to be. He admired the house, and the seat in the sun by the back door, and the cows, and he smiled at the members of the family as they passed into and out of the house. 'Poor soul,' said Mam, 'he looks lost.' Even Aunt Kate took to him and it was she who suggested the loft over the stable.

He became one of our household, accepted, expected, depended on. He occupied, however, an undefined place, not family, not employee, in a gap between the grown-ups and us youngest ones, Joe, Mollie, me and Dan. He was a grown-up of course, in fact to us he seemed quite old, but unlike the other men he did not spend his days working on the land, and so spent a lot of his time with us. He seemed to enjoy that, and so did we.

Many of our outings took us along the Old Road, which was a lane that had once been the principal road to Town, but was now narrowed by hawthorns and hazels and used only by people on foot or by horses. At the first bridge, we crossed the slopey field to the stream that came down from the mountain. We pushed between the tall hazel rods that separated our fields from the scrubland, and were in a dim sun-dappled place under a grove of fir-trees. At our feet the little stream tumbled over rocks and moss. We made boats, sailed them across Atlantic pools and over Niagarous rapids, made dams and harbours, bridges and mill wheels. Rich sat nearby, that was his part in our play. He had a gift of not imposing himself on a situation, he was interested but not in any way critical. We were glad to know he was there, a happy presence that did not inhibit our fun.

I remember from those times how sparkling clean the air was, and the water in the stream.

Or we might go further along the Old Road to the house where our parents had lived before any of us were born. Others had taken their place; the last member of that family married, the wedding party went on for a week until every scrap of food and drink was gone and every song had been sung, and then the dancing had to stop, they turned the key in the door and went to America, leaving the empty house to fall into ruin. We always went to the doorway and looked in but we

were a bit scared of it and of the jackdaws that flew up from
the chimney and talked and squabbled. Fascinated, we had to
go and see it, but frightened too, and usually very quiet as we
went away.

Rich did his best to help around the place, bringing water
from the well, or sometimes scuffling the gravel in Aunt
Kate's garden, but she couldn't trust him to do any weeding.
'He doesn't know a flower from a weed,' she used say indignantly. He was very dependable at making sure all the hens
and turkeys were safe at nightfall, in case the fox was on the
prowl. He was willing to do any errand, to go to the shop or
the post office. In our house, of course, there was no scarcity
of messengers unless it was in school-time, so it usually meant
that Rich and one or two of us went, and on the way there
would be adventures – tadpoles, or chestnuts in the autumn, or
hiding in the tree near the school and watching the passers-by,
or being chased by Malone's wicked dog, or building a dam
on Whelan's stream to make the water run out across the field.
He didn't play a very active part, but acted as a look-out and
he could be depended on completely if there were secrets to
be kept. Although Mam always told us not to delay, we often
stopped a while at the cross. We sat on the three big flat stones
at the corner and watched who went by, on foot or on carts. I
remember how smooth and shiny those three stones were and
I realize now why they were like that: it was because they had
been polished by the many spectators who had used them as a
grandstand during pitch-and-toss schools, or a bit of hurling
or football. After Mass on fine Sundays, people sat there to

talk, or smoke their pipes; there was always someone there. It was a meeting place; Rich said it was the centre of the parish.

Once in a while, a policeman used cycle out from town but he could be seen coming along the straight stretch of road, and there was plenty of time for the pitch-and-toss players to scatter, usually up past the graveyard, through the Priest's field, to the upper road. On one occasion that was long remembered, he outflanked the gamblers by turning up past the forge and coming down unexpectedly on them by way of Nolan's Lane. Most of them escaped through Lizzie Nolan's garden, but he captured two, gave them a severe lecture, and worst of all confiscated a penny from each of them. As he was about to remount his bicycle, however, he stopped and called them, handed back their money and said, 'You're to put those in the priest's box on Sunday. Do you hear me now! Without fail! I'll be talking to Fr Doyle about it.'

That had happened before Rich came into our lives, and when we told him about it, he surprised us when he said, 'Served them right!'

'Why, Rich? People always played pitch-and-toss there.'

'Because it's illegal.'

'But why?'

'It's an insult to the queen's image,' and when he saw that we didn't understand, he said, 'Don't you know the queen's head is on every coin?' I suppose we did know that; anyway as none of us had a coin to demonstrate what Rich was telling us, he put two fingers into one of his waistcoat pockets, took out a small string-bag, opened it carefully and shook out into his palm some tiny silver coins. He wouldn't let us handle them but he let us look at them closely; we had seen threepenny bits before, of course, but there were also tiny silver pennies and two-penny pieces. 'Look at the queen's head,' and then put them with great care back in the bag, tightened the cord and stowed it again in his pocket.

'Why did you never spend them, Rich?'

He looked a bit shocked. 'Oh no, I couldn't spend those. They were a present from Mrs Bannerman. She was a lovely lady. She said they were a thank you for bringing the family to so many lovely places and bringing them safe home again. And that was only a year before she died. And she was young. Her husband went off to his house in England after that and never came back to Ireland. Her little baby died the same time and they were buried together in the one grave.'

I wanted to ask him if those were really silver buttons on his waistcoat, and were they a uniform, and if they were, was it because he was a coachman, but just then he stood up, and said something about seeing to the horses and walked away from us. This was more information than we'd ever got, up to then, about Rich's former life. We surmised that that might have been when he lost his job as coachman.

Joe said, 'I think he's sad talking about Mrs Bannerman and the baby.'

This strange man was completely dependent on my parents' goodness of heart, and was very conscious and appreciative of that, yet with a gentle unassuming dignity and a pride in his skill and knowledge. He was just different, with an air about

him of being part of a world beyond our experience, a suggestion of mystery and otherness. His influence did not depend
on his having authority. He was simply Rich.

He hadn't the skill or the strength for farm work, knew
nothing about it, which was strange until we found that he never
had worked on a farm and that his gifts were really in his dealings
with the two plough-horses and the pony. Never had they been
better cared for, never had they looked so well; he was happy
to spend hours brushing and grooming them, talking quietly,
whether to himself or to the horses we couldn't tell, or whistling tunelessly; never had they been so petted and loved. In the
coldest of the winter he slept in the centre stall in the stable, the
horses in the two outer stalls, plenty of straw and hay, a blanket
that Aunt Kate had found for him and patched, an old cast-off
overcoat of Daddy's. If he couldn't sleep he talked to the horses.
'No, it doesn't disturb them. When they're asleep they don't hear
me and if they're awake they always agree with me.'

Some of our neighbours must have wondered at Mam
taking in this stray. I overheard two women talking after Mass
one Sunday, 'Hasn't she enough to do with that houseful,
without takin' in another. And a stranger, no kith or kin' – but
Mam didn't think like that. If she stopped to think about it
at all, it was probably, 'Well, there's fifteen in this house. One
more won't make much difference.' Once I heard my cousin
Tim's mother saying that Mam took in Rich to fill the gaps
in her life that her dead children had left. Another Joe – there
were two Joes in our family, he was the second eldest boy –
died the same year as Margaret who died as an infant, and

Mam's mother, our Granny, died the year after. Maybe Rich did fill some gap in a wounded heart.

There must have been many wet days but the fine sunny days are the ones I remember. On wet days, if the hay wasn't in, we could play marbles in the hay-barn, or football if there was room, or we might be told by Daddy to clean out the stable or one of the calf-houses. We made things, toys and gadgets, in the car-shed, out of bits of iron or timber or whatever we could find. Anyone who had a penknife sharpened it on the stone, and carved things. I remember one wet day when we were perched on the two common cars in the car-shed, looking out at the rain and the puddles and the dripping trees, and Rich asked about the Old House. He wanted us to tell him again about it, as if the sadness of it troubled him, maybe with memories of his own.

But even on really cold wet days we could make ourselves cosy in the hay and listen to Rich talking. He told us about the coach-horses he used to drive for the Bannermans. The coach-horses had magic names, Prince and Beauty, Black Bob and Blazer, and there was a coach and four. The Bannermans were big people, with a house in England as well as in Ireland. But they were Irish, too, because one of the Bannermans had married an O'Moore lady, and he told us about the banshee that cried about the woods or on the turrets of the big house when one of the family was going to die. 'The banshee follows the O'Moores,' he told us. After that, any time I heard the voice of the snipe, the *gabhairín reo*, like a goat in the April twilight, I pretended it was the banshee. I half-believed it, and always hurried home. The marshy land by the stream at the bottom of Knockeen hill was where the snipe lived and where the dusk smelled of garlic in April. And wasn't it strange that garlic was what kept you safe from banshees and other bad things like that, so Rich told us.

He told us about the forty-eight horses, the coach-horses that he loved best of all, hunters too, work-horses and polo ponies, and he explained how polo was played. I think we hardly believed him, yet if Rich said so, it must be true. There were fifty rooms in the big house and a hundred windows. But we boasted that our house was where the landlord lived before he went to live in one of his other houses, and that he had made big changes, for instance what we called the front door had once opened into the farmyard, but he put the farm-yard around at the back and built all the stone and slated out-houses. And we emphasised to Rich that an *Architect* had been employed to see to all those changes. We thought he would be impressed to hear that, but he paid little heed to it and we were disappointed. It was difficult to interest him in other things, apart from horses.

I recall very vividly an incident that happened one October night when, just before bedtime, Rich called us, Mollie, Dan and me, Joe being away, and asked us if we'd like to see the Hunter's Moon. We had never heard of it before, so of course we went with him, not sure what to expect. There wasn't a cloud in the dark overhead; there wasn't a breath of wind. He led us past the Grove and pointed to the gap between the two old pine-trees. One tree was in darkness, the other bright and shining, and out beyond, watching us from the unclouded sky was a great yellow bowl of creamy moon, smiling and calm. Rich said, 'That's the Hunter's Moon' and he said it proudly, as if he regarded it as *his* moon. Mollie put her arms around me and Dan and we gazed at it in an awed silence. Sometimes I think I can still see the three small children standing in the moonlight between the tall pines and gazing at the biggest, roundest, yellowest moon that ever was.

The years went by, and I grew taller, and so did Joe and Mollie and Dan. Everyone else seemed to stay the same. Rich, anyway, didn't change: Daddy tried to get him to whitewash the house and the lawn-piers, but he wasn't good at it, and splashed the whitewash onto the windows and the sills. He had that one great gift, he could talk to horses. I think Daddy was a bit cross with him, but he was never cross for long, and Mam said, 'Everybody has one gift, and you can't expect more.' The upshot of it was that it was left like that: anything to do with horses or transport, but little else, was Rich's business. Other farmers around took to calling to ask his advice about sick horses or other animals, and we were proud of his reputation.

It was a big change when Joe went away to boarding school. I remember that year well because it was the year Frances died. She was only seventeen, a pale quiet girl who seldom came out to join in our games, but helped Aunt Kate in the house. She didn't talk much, ever, but at times she would surprise you with a sudden shy smile that lighted up her face and that vanished again as quickly as it came. I can't explain how I felt when she died, why I didn't grieve more. I was more confused than sad. Our house was full of weeping. One day I came on Mamie and Jo with their arms around each other, crying, not saying anything, just crying, and I could not join in their grief. What I remember most is how small and still and white she looked in the big bed where she was waked. And the white roses, I remember that. And the way the candle flames jumped when someone knelt down to say a prayer at her bed. Now I watched the grave, still face on the pillow, the face that was, and was not, my sister; I knew that that face would never again light up with her little fugitive smile.

Though I was only twelve, I began then to understand that the one who had died had indeed gone to where there was no more sorrow, leaving us to cope with the absence and loss. It was my first encounter with the great mystery. There was a queer empty feeling about the house after she was gone, and a silence. Rich behaved very strangely; he would not go to the funeral but sulked and gloomed for a long while afterwards and then he took to going to her grave and staying there for ages, just thinking or saying his prayers. Or was he telling her he was sorry for not being there to say goodbye for the last time? Or explaining that he could not bear to see her put down into the wet clay? Then he came to Mam and Daddy and asked to be forgiven for his behaviour. Of course he was forgiven; they knew he loved all of us children, but that Frances was the one he had loved best.

One life had ended, and, it seemed for just a little while, so had ours; but life went on, as always. Slowly, with reluctance almost, but inevitably. Duties forced us to think of other things.

On Pattern Day every year all the family went to the churchyard; we tidied the graves and put flowers on them. Rich was
left at home in charge; he was pleased and proud at being
trusted and depended on. In the long summer days Mam and
Daddy often went out after the evening meal; they gathered
a bunch of roses from the orchard hedge and we knew where
they were going. It was important that the bridge be held
between the living and the dead.

The corn was always brought to Mullenbeg to be ground.
I often went there and I knew it well. Especially I remember
the last time Rich and I went. He and I set off, down the
hill, along the New Road and so down the leafy lane till we
reached the mill, shady under the trees. Rich, as he always did,
sat up very straight and held the reins high as I suppose he
had held them when he drove Bannerman's horses. When the
meal was ready and loaded, Rich handed me the reins. I was
delighted. I was well able to manage our horses – I was sixteen
then – but Rich had never before allowed me to drive if he was
with me. So I held the reins high, like him, and said, 'Ho, hup,
there, Dick,' in imitation.

I hoped Rich would praise my driving, but he didn't; in
fact I remember now that he was very quiet on the way home,
though I didn't notice at the time. When we got home, we
lifted out the sacks together and I helped him to unyoke the
horse. But as he and I lifted the heavy collar up onto the
wooden peg on the stable wall, he stumbled, fell against the
wall and to my consternation slid slowly down till he lay in a
funny shape on the straw and cobbles.

I ran to the house and Mam came back with me. 'Get Lar and Jim. They're in the hay-barn.' When the three of us got back, Mam and Aunt Kate had put Rich sitting against the stable wall and he had come to. He insisted he was better and asked to be carried up to his bed over the stable. Aunt Kate prepared hot milk and goody and I was told to look out for him and make sure he was all right and to get him anything he wanted. He didn't complain, but he seemed very weak and all the fight had gone out of him. The priest came to see him next day, and afterwards he conferred with Mam and Daddy and I heard some of what he said: 'He's very weak and resigned ... it's as if he knew ... he's all prepared to go anyway ... maybe the doctor ... but I don't know ... said I was to thank you for ... he was very anxious that I'd tell you that.' I didn't like hearing them talk like that, I didn't want to believe he was very sick.

In ones and twos we went to see him. He smiled and shook hands with everyone, and thanked us over and over, and in an old-fashioned way he kissed Mam's and Aunt Kate's hands. I couldn't believe but that he would be well in a day or two. No matter what I was doing, I remembered to go to see if he needed anything; I'd go to the middle rung of the stairs and from there I could see his bed, and if he was asleep I wouldn't disturb him. Aunt Kate made hot drinks for him, and food that she thought he might like, but he ate very little. When I did speak to him, he took my hand, and spoke about 'all the adventures'. His voice was weak and he stopped often as if to get his breath.

Late on the day after the priest's visit, I went to check on him as usual. I went halfway up the stairs and looked across at his bed. He seemed to be sleeping. I turned to go down again, when a noise made me look back, and I saw him suddenly sit up very straight. He held up his two hands in that way he had of holding the reins and in a loud clear voice said, 'Ho, hup, there! Pick'em up, boy! Hup, you beauty!' and shook the reins and flicked his long whip, and then fell back on his pillow, and I knew he was dead. Don't ask me how, but I knew. And even stranger than that, I wasn't afraid, though I had never before seen anyone die. I think the reason I wasn't afraid was that he looked so happy, as if his last journey had brought him to a place of shining peace.

Flight

The great sea-loch was dark and silent under a clouded sky. It was not, however, empty of human presence and activity. Near the loch's outlet to the sea, in the black shadow of the hills, a ship tugged at its anchor, in an ebbing sea and a faint offshore breeze. There were muted noises and whispered words as the oarsmen took their places in the longboat at the ship's side, pushed away, and quickly settled to a steady rhythm.

The steersman made for the slack water in the lee of the headland. Progress there was quicker, but all his skill was needed to avoid hazards of rocks and shallows, even with the aid of the sharp eyes of the boy sitting in the bow. It was the first of the many journeys they must make from their vessel to the jetty on the western shore; experience gained from this first attempt would make later crossings easier, but while caution and silence were necessary, no time must be lost if their ship with its full complement on board was to clear the harbour-mouth before the turn of the tide.

A seabird, startled from its night-roost, flew up suddenly and wheeled away in raucous protest. At once the oarsmen lowered their hands, thus lifting the blades out of the water, and all waited in tense silence. Waited while the bird's desolate cry faded into the night. No word was said, and for minutes they remained so, silent and motionless, while the water slapped against the bow and slow drops fell from the oars.

But the longboat lost way, swinging towards the land, and when their keel scraped on a hidden rock they were obliged to resume rowing. The tension ended only when the helmsman saw with relief the raised arm of his lookout-boy gesturing shoreward; his keen young eyes had found the one tiny light in that wilderness of dark.

The watcher by the pier, eyes grown accustomed to the dim light, could see the track that began at the water's edge and straggled up and around the cluster of houses, the track by which he and the others had come; he could hear the lap of water against stone, the distant bark of a dog, the nearer whinny of one of their tired horses, stabled behind the houses; he could see in imagination the dark hull and the bare masts and yards of the ship that lurked near the mouth of the loch.

Then a new sound, of oars dipped quietly by practised hands, a long-awaited welcome sound. He went to the door of the nearest house and knocked softly. The candle in the window at once was quenched, the door opened and the first group made their cautious way down towards the jetty.

To this ignominy the great princes had come, forced to skulk furtively under cover of night, in the land where once they ruled.

At midnight the vessel slipped away on the last of the ebb, rounding Fanad to face the anger of the Atlantic, and the fugitives began their long journey into exile.

All the Spangled Host

'Come quick, Golly! Quails! On the lawn! Quick.' The urgency in Berry's voice roused me at once from my chair. I saw with surprise that it was growing dark – how long had I been dozing?

There was no sign of the girls but Colm stood looking out through the bars of the fence into Finneran's field. 'Where are Berry and Aileen?'

'In the field. They ran after the birds.'

He came skipping across the lawn and took my hand. 'The stars are coming out, Golly. Look!' He flopped down on his back. 'This is where you see them best. Come and look,' so we lay side by side on the grass and watched and wondered. Above us the glittering heaven. What was Milton's word to describe the starry sky? We've named some of the stars and galaxies, tamed them as we think, although if we tamed ten thousand more the percentage of known in the total would still be zero. Illimitable! 'Spangled!' – that was Milton's word.

The sky slowly darkened, and as the stars' cold heat burned off the shreds of mist and cloud, so the stars themselves burned brighter. Infinity! We know so little; the Greeks knew as much. The Arabs, too, studied the stars, brilliant men such as Maimonides. Aldebaran sounds Arabic. The Egyptians, the Sumerians. And even the nameless people who built long before the pyramids but had no means of passing on their knowledge other than their great stone monument on the Boyne. All these came, learned and went, their knowledge often lost to succeeding times. So why that odd assumption that man is on an inevitably upward path towards understanding, wisdom, betterment? We are now so sure that we know it all, arrogant in our mastery of technology. But wisdom?

'Why do they wink?' he interrupted my thoughts, and I was unable to tell him.

'Maybe,' I suggested, 'they are little young stars, like you; they know you are watching them, so they wink at you.' He seemed to like that idea.

I had been neglecting my duties. 'We must see if the two girls are back.'

'Oh they are, Golly. They came back along the lane. They're in the kitchen.' So, all accounted for. I relaxed.

They *do* wink. Why? Some of them, we are told, are still twinkling though they no longer exist, their light still on its way to us although the source of that light died long ago. Dead stars that shine brightly, just like Shakespeare or Rubens or Mozart.

He raised himself on his elbows. 'Will Daddy and Mammy bring the new baby home tomorrow?'

'They will of course.' He jumped up. I got to my feet, too, but more slowly.

'Golly, what will we call him?'

'Mammy and Daddy will know. What would you like?'

'Dan. Or maybe Billy. What would you like, Golly?'

'Maimonides.' He looked up, startled, and knew by my smile that I was joking. He repeated the big word carefully, pronouncing it as I had done. He already had an ear and a liking for words. 'Anyway, whatever we call him, he will always be your pal.'

'Yes,' he said solemnly, 'always.' He had another question, 'Who is Maimonides?'

'He was a very clever Arab who lived long ago.'

'A real Arab? Like the one on his camel, in my book?'

'Yes,' I agreed, though with reservations.

'Now it's time for your supper. I must get your sisters', too; it's time you were all in bed.'

'Can I have two bickies?'

'Of course.'

I peeped in the open door of the girls' room. Berry and Aileen lay on their stomachs on the carpet, propped on their elbows, kicking their heels, looking at a big book. Berry said, 'See, they *were* quails.' I think she was determined that they should be quail, maybe she liked the sound of the word.

I knocked. 'Come along, girls. Time for supper. If your Mammy knew how late I let you stay up, she'd be cross.'

'Can we watch TV, Golly? Please!'

I looked at my watch. 'Well, all right. Twenty minutes, that's all.'

'Golly, can we make hot chocolate?'

'Do you know how?'

'Course we do,' and I watched, fearful of accidents, but I needn't have worried.

'Now drink that while you watch the television.'

Colm was struggling into his nightclothes. I made him comfortable in his bed, read the story he wanted, about a young frog that couldn't swim and had to have swimming lessons from a seal (it didn't work out very well, the seal had never heard of legs). He was grappling with a serious question: 'Can unicorns fly? Ber says they can.' My answer had to be carefully considered. 'Big sisters are usually right. I've never seen a unicorn that couldn't fly,' wondering if he would see the ambiguity in that, but it seemed to satisfy him. At any rate, he fell asleep almost at once.

They were still watching the TV. 'Oh, you rascals! Switch that off. It's long past bed-time.'

'But, Golly, it's not over yet. Another five minutes. Please?'

So what could I do? When the programme ended, 'Now wash those cups and then bed.'

They seemed rather astonished at being expected to wash their cups, probably thinking, 'What are dishwashers for?' but did so without complaint.

When they had gone to their room, after a lengthy washing of teeth and a visit to the sitting room to see if the quail had returned, I was glad of my comfortable armchair again. Not wishing to read, I left the room in darkness, moved my chair closer to the window.

The garden gleamed faintly, lit by its million candles.

Why had Maimonides come to mind? In Córdoba we had

stayed in the Hotel Maimonides; the name meant nothing to me then, but close by was the great mosque, and there our guide spoke of the noted philosopher. To simplify my story I had told the little boy that Maimonides was an Arab; it might have been more accurate to say a Moor or a Spaniard; yet most know him as Jewish. To me he seems to be simply Mediterranean, and I imagined our guide in the mosque to be another such, in fact not another but the same; I began to think of him, still think of him, as Maimonides, as a personification of the Mediterranean with its inextricable mixture of races. He was urbane, sardonic, dark, stocky in build, a southern head, brachycephalic, quite unlike the long-headed Celt. He spoke knowledgeably of the Goats and the Visigoats (Goths, we assumed). Speaking to us among many other groups of tourists, he had difficulty in making himself heard, and glanced several times with increasing exasperation at a loud-voiced guide nearby; he tried to continue, but eventually gave up, and, for that moment abandoning his civilized polish, turned towards the noisy one and snarled, 'Shut up!' The other paid not the slightest attention. Our man looked at us, shrugged elaborately and hissed, 'Germans!' I noticed in his lapel a small Star of David brooch. Was he, I wondered, thinking of the very different treatment of Jews by the Germans and by the notably tolerant Moors? Long memories, old grievances. (Or was that little scene between the two guides enacted for the entertainment of the tourists?)

That face and head could have been that of Alexander, or of Cosimo, who may have been Etruscan, or of 'that talkative bald-headed seaman' returning to Ithaca by devious ways from Troy. It could have been that of a Pharaoh, or of Hannibal, or of any one individual in the teeming seaports of Marseilles, Venice, Istanbul. Or might not Vasco have had such a face, or Cristobal Colon, or Marco Polo who found a way of linking the two great seedbeds of modern civilization, that of India and China in the far east, separated by seas, mountains and deserts from the other, the Fertile Crescent and the fringes of the Mediterranean. The Golden Road, that one thin silken thread that tied East to West, no road at all but a series of migration trails made by wild horses, ancestors of all our horses, as they searched for grazing and water. Imagine the thunder of hooves and the flying manes as they drove in their thousands through the passes of the Tien Shan. Imagine the hardihood and daring of those 'Merchant Princes of Baghdad', braving deserts, snow-capped mountains, robbers, flood drought and storm, hunger and thirst, to bring back the riches of the fabulous Orient, those masters of the long caravans laden with silk and spices, porcelain and lapis lazuli, more precious than gold, while somewhere in one of those bales, smuggled out of China, were silkworms, hidden in a bamboo tube. And all that fierce activity and enterprise to serve the needs and wants of the brilliant civilizations bordering the Mediter- ranean, civilizations that reached upriver along the Nile and the Danube, east to the Euphrates and Persia, north and west to the islands of the western sea.

Europe has left us far behind in the waves and mists of the Atlantic, fighting stubbornly for our lives, for our very survival as the last Celtic civilization on earth, and as a result of that long struggle with our nearest neighbour we have only a slight acquaintance with European culture.

The chiming clock on the mantelpiece brought me back from my wandering. It was time to call Jim on his mobile for his latest news. He was in his room at Hale's, had just arrived from the hospital. 'All well, wonderfully well, both asleep before I left. Home early afternoon tomorrow. I'll ring before we start.' Jim is a good fellow; I could smile now remembering our doubts – Marie's and mine – when Grace and he had first met; not unusual, I suppose, for parents to think that no man is good enough for their daughter. I went then to see the children. They were sound asleep. I watched them for a long moment, listened to their quiet breathing. 'Trailing clouds of glory do we come.'

The carton of chocolate was still on the kitchen table. I read the instructions, which seemed to be quite simple, so following them carefully I succeeded in making my first mug of drinking chocolate. It looked and smelled delicious. Very proud, I carried the steaming mug to my chair near the garden window.

But as I went to sit down, something – a movement, a change in the light – caught my attention. Very slowly and quietly I reached for the binoculars on the window-ledge. Yes, they were back, I could make out two of them, and as far as my limited knowledge went, quail, so Berry had been right. What had attracted them there? After being startled away from it earlier? My guess was the coiled spring-loaded seed-pods of cyclamen under the birch trees. They are not night-birds. But had this exceptional night, gleaming like jewel, tempted them?

They were busy, heads down, intent, untroubled by any sense of danger, unaware of being observed, unaware of the privilege they had granted me. For a long time I stood watching, and

I thought how unimportant are material things compared with the simple priceless gifts of life: the sky and its wonders, the inoffensive small creatures of the wilderness under the starlit night. The innocence of children, and sleep, and dream.

Long Odds

Ours is a small office, but interesting things happen there. That Tuesday, for instance, I believe it was the week before Fairyhouse ...

Viney saw him first, and immediately disappeared. She couldn't stand him, couldn't stand the sight of him. Viney, you understand, was like that; there were very few people she could stand the sight of, and besides, the first sight of Johnny Bourke that Tuesday clearly said trouble.

Our only other customer that slack morning (customer is not quite the right word, but let it be) was little Miss Gabard, who calls at least once every day, and, no, she doesn't have an account with us but just likes to be sure that we are all well. Seeing the gathering storm-clouds, she thought it best to go, as quietly as she had come, to await a more opportune time. I walked with her to the door and thanked her for calling. 'Perhaps a later time,' I suggested. She adjusted her spectacles and blinked up at me. 'You are very kind, Mr Widger. I am glad to see you looking so well,' and left, no doubt to attend to other pressing business.

Poll Hamilton, tiny, quiet, and afraid of no one, was left to face the storm. He demanded, loudly and luridly, to see the manager, the assistant manager, the cashier, the half-eejit responsible for dishonouring his cheque, all of whose antecedents he appeared to hold in very low esteem. He stopped short of calling for heads on platters, but he did convey his opinions with impressive eloquence. I must say I was proud of him.

Poll tried to explain, and her explanation involved the word Reconciliation, a word everyone knows, but bankers have their own specialized meaning for it. Johnny wasn't having any: 'Reconciliation my arse, there'll be no reconciliation here,' whacked the counter with his stick, and left. He did his best to slam the door behind him. The door, however, was fastened to the wall by a hook; he pulled the hook out of the wall and a strip of timber with it. There was a tearing, splintering noise that was drowned by the crash of the door closing.

After which, a breathless silence.

Someone went to re-open the door, while the manager wrung his hands and Dermot said darkly, 'Bygod he wouldn't do that in my office,' Viney disapproved icily of everything and everyone, while Poll and the new girl, Claire, rolled on the cubicle floor, crying down salt tears of pure happiness and trying to pull lumps out of the carpet. The only practical thing I could think of was to switch off the alarm and then ring the Garda Barrack to explain. Big Jim Mullins answered the phone and I told him all was well, just some slight collateral damage and no fatalities. He inquired especially about Viney's well-being. I think he fancied her, the attraction of the iceberg for the Titanic. Well, she's a fine girl, even if a bit on the far side of distant.

And wouldn't you guess? Johnny was back later in the day with smiles and chocolates, and a shady story for Dermot which he told at the top of his voice so that everyone could enjoy it. There were free passes, too, for the next meeting at the Junction. He slapped a round brown parcel on the counter in front of Poll Hamilton. 'I got it in Jimmy Sheridan's. It's for you. He hadn't any flowers.' It was a big yellow melon. Viney, coming back from the post office, was caught in the open near the manager's room. Johnny whirled on her and gave her a smack on the rump that nearly lifted her onto the counter, then drew himself up and said, 'All friends here!' smiled his big smile and left all of us smiling too. All except Viney, of course.

That was Tuesday, a slow day. Maybe you thought banking was a boring job?

The day of Johnny's wedding brought us all together again. Many changes in the meantime. Mr Widger, our manager then, now retired, looked so well that I hardly knew him; he looked as if the weight of half a century had been lifted from his shoulders. Dermot, now manager somewhere in North Tipp, was thinner than I remembered; too much golf, and bridge, and trying to keep the bosses happy. He confided in me that he had chronic indigestion. Poll Hamilton brought her bright face from Head Office, but she looked more serious, less bubbly; Head Office is no laughing matter and doesn't encourage bubbly. Claire had married and brought her new husband along. Johnny, slightly rounder, slightly redder, welcomed us all and seemed rather surprised but certainly delighted that all of us had turned up. I was officially at that time assistant manager, but in fact I was running the place. I'm one of those awkward employees who don't want promotion but can't be done without (though sometimes I suspect they'd be glad to get rid of me). I never applied for promotion but I know more about the job than all the rest of them put together, and especially more than poor Hayden who has been manager here for twelve months and still knows none of the customers; he's not over-bright, though a nice poor fellow.

Now who have I forgotten? Viney of course. Dear Viney! She didn't look as if she enjoyed crowds, but she did her best; at some time that day I actually saw her smile. But then the bride is expected to smile. Oh yes! Did I forget to tell you? Viney and Johnny. Hard to believe, isn't it? Twelve months ago who in his sober senses would have bet on a Bourke-Viney double? Even though at that time the odds would have been more than generous. But there you are — the Glorious Uncertainty.

And I was largely responsible. I've been here so long that I know everyone within thirty miles of this town — everyone. *And* their parents, and their children, and all belonging to them. I've told you I think that Viney didn't care much for people. But she loves horses. And Johnny Bourke *owns* horses. One day at Gowran Park I happened on her in the crowd and asked her if she'd like to meet some of the owners. She was only thrilled. Things moved on rapidly from there until in April Johnny told her that he had a horse running at Punchestown, that he and Ted Faulkner and Edie were driving up and would Viney like to come. It was an invitation she found impossible to refuse. So she had the hair done and bought herself a fancy hat, put on her finery, went to Punchestown and had a ball, rubbing shoulders, elbows, hips even (dare I mention thighs?) with owners and breeders and trainers and jockeys, and decided there and then that she had at last found her proper environment. Johnny's horse didn't win, but Johnny did.

Viney got home from Punchestown very late, very happy, more than a little tipsy, a bit vague about some of the day's happenings but convinced of one thing: this was the life she had known to be her destiny and her due, ever since her schooldays and those classes at Miss McCool's Equestrian Academy. Her father had been appalled at the cost, but now it began to look as if the classes had been a bargain.

Everyone will have an opinion on the matter. Was it a match made in heaven? If it wasn't it was pretty close, it was a match made at the races, and for many people that's as near to heaven as makes no odds.

In the middle of all the connubiality of Johnny and Viney's big day, I was occupied with an idea, prompted I daresay by my part in bringing them together: banking is not as sound and secure a profession as it used to be, and I'm still half-thinking of setting up a Lonely Hearts agency somewhere in this locality. Just as a side-line. It seems to have possibilities, even in hard times.

A Night Bird

Among our summer bird visitors is one that few people in Ireland have heard and fewer have seen. Yet in those times when country people knew more about their surroundings, this bird had a part in their knowledge and their folklore, and they knew it well enough to have given it several names, some accurately descriptive, one bordering on defamatory. Its most usual name is Nightjar or Nightchurr, an attempt to describe its strange call. It is a bird of the dusk, like the owl, and indeed one of its old names in England is Fern-owl. Another is Dor-hawk. It is, however, neither owl nor hawk but is kin to the swift. The Irish name is *Túirne Lín*, meaning Spinning-wheel or Flax-wheel, again a reference to its voice. This little-known and rather mysterious bird is also called Goatsucker, though it has nothing to do with goats, in spite of its Latin name *Caprimulgus*, its food being moths and other insects of the night.

In 1943, when Irish roads had little tarmac on them and less wheeled traffic, I bought a second-hand Raleigh bicycle for £10.

I needed it for my work. Provided I could get an occasional tyre and tube and an inch or two of valve rubber, I was king of the road. Even on my seventy-mile round trip to my parents' home at weekends, I seldom saw a car or lorry or tractor.

Cycling one summer's night along a level road that I knew well, through an area of marshy fields with tussocks of rushes, royal fern and dwarf willows, I heard a sound I had never heard before but that I recognized at once. If I had turned my bicycle upside down on the handlebars and saddle (which I often had to do because of punctures), then given the front wheel a brisk turn and held a twig against the spokes, the sound produced would have been reminiscent of the sound I heard from the marshland, a continuous whirring that suggested a mechanical rather than a natural origin.

Leaving my bicycle against a gate, I climbed over and began to make my way towards the sound. I had been cycling for nearly half an hour and my eyes had become accustomed to the darkness, and though there was neither moon nor stars I could find my way without too much difficulty. I went slowly and as quietly as I could, avoiding clumps, pools and bushes. Knowing that the Nightjar may sing in flight I sometimes scanned the sky but without seeing any bird. The voice in any case seemed to come always from the same spot and I went in that general direction. My progress was steady if slow. Once I looked back but could not see gate or bicycle or road.

I stopped to consider: should I continue right up to him, startle him into flight and hope that he would be clearly visible against the sky, or proceed even more stealthily and pause at a distance of two or three yards when I might see him where he crouched and sang? Either way I now began to realize my chance of a clear sighting of my quarry was small enough. Undecided, I lifted my right foot to take another step, when, as though on that signal, the churring stopped.

There followed a blank, baffling silence, unbroken by a bird's cry, by a moth's flutter, by a beetle's hum. The night was empty. No wing or throat to guide my further progress, and without his voice, I could no longer determine with any clarity where he had been. I had lost him — or more accurately, he had lost me. To be as close as that, and my chance was gone of meeting that elusive hunter of the night sky, that nocturnal mocker. I was standing on one leg in a boggy field, while he watched and no doubt laughed up his sleeve.

I turned back disconsolately, for the first time aware that one foot was wringing wet from stepping in a bog-pool. Now that that insistent whirring had ceased I began to hear the other noises. We tend to think of the night as a time of quiet and stillness, a time of sleep. But the night has its own life. A faint breeze moved the grass. A beetle blundered into my face, startling me. From the hill a fox barked, and when I stopped and listened, there were rustling sounds made by small night-creatures. The air was full of voices.

Having found my way to where I had left my bicycle, I climbed to the top of the gate and turned to look back, when right on cue, that mocking song began once more. He was laughing at me, chuckling in that strange purring voice made of moth, cobweb, twilight, under every bush, under no bush, out there somewhere in his familiar friendly darkness.

Reinforcements

There had been no notice of Larry Somers's death in the daily papers, and so I missed his funeral. However, a man of his age who had enjoyed life must not be mourned. Eighty-six, he had told me, and still well able to be out and about, going regularly to do a bit of salmon-fishing on the Slaney, visiting the children and grandchildren and great-grandchildren, having a drink and a game of cards with the cronies. That information I had from him two months before he died, when we met in the Oak Tavern, beside the river he loved. It was on that occasion also that he told me a little story that has stuck in my memory.

When he was a small boy, just started school, his family lived beside the main road between Rosslare and Wexford town. His father worked as a groom on the estate of a big landowner.

Very early one morning of the school holidays, the boy ran out the front door of his home, barefoot, to meet the day's adventures. Almost at once he was back again in high excitement, shouting, 'Mammy, Mammy, the horses are after gettin' out. Tell Daddy.'

The mother said, 'Are you sure, Larry?' took his hand and

went with him to the gate, and they looked down the road to the south. Coming towards them out of the morning mist there were indeed horses, but it was very soon clear that these were not from the estate, and that each one had a rider. The horses came on slowly, their heads down, their reins slack, the riders swaying a little from side to side, and the boy was frightened by these animals that clearly were horses but did not behave like the tall hunters he knew, and by the men who seemed to him not to be alive, so that he took his mother's hand and pulled her back into the doorway of their house. They watched in awe as the long line passed, and saw that the men wore military uniforms and were armed with rifles. A long cavalcade, hundreds of them, and no human voice, just the clop of hooves on the dusty road, the creak of harness, the clink of a chain.

The boy and his mother watched them pass, and now they knew why there were no voices and why the riders swayed: every soldier was asleep in the saddle. Someone who knows more about such things must tell me if it is possible to sleep while riding a horse, but that's the story as Larry told it to me. They had had an uncomfortable crossing by the night ferry from Wales, and were catching up on their sleep. The two watchers stayed until the last soldier had passed, and waited and watched still until all had disappeared from sight.

Where had these ghostly riders come from, and where were they going? They had, of course, come from barracks somewhere in Britain to embark at Fishguard Harbour, and having landed at Rosslare in the early hours of the morning, were headed for Wexford barracks, on the first stage of their journey to Dublin. It was Easter Week, 1916.

Remembering Derrynane

To our right the mountain lifted abruptly in dripping stone and bog and heather. The Scarriff Inn clung precariously to the opposite edge of the road and, beyond it, the land fell away as steeply, then less steeply, into small fields that ended at the rocky margin of the Atlantic.

Having left our luggage at the Inn, we wandered down a winding by-road towards the sea, the evening sun still warm. A grove of wind-shorn trees by the water's edge sheltered a house, home of a noted sailor. Sheep grazed the little slanting fields. In the hedges and on the warm stones butterflies basked, Clouded Yellows, continental visitors that often come in autumn to this mild west coast; they were here in numbers, quite content it seemed, little disturbed, easy to catch; when I opened my cupped hands again the beautiful creature did not fly away but lazily spread its wings to the sunlight, unalarmed.

This is a place of splendid sunsets, also of splendid storms, open to the worst the angry ocean can throw at it, and in the long ago many a Spanish wine-ship arriving here at nightfall must have been glad to follow the guiding lights that showed the way to secure anchorage, maybe in the lee of Abbey Island or some other sheltered inlet, safe from storm and exciseman. That was then, when O'Connells ruled here.

Night closed the butterflies' yellow wings, morning brought again the gift of sunshine. The hostelry was bright and sunfilled, but oddly, no one was about, no host or hostess, no evidence of cooking. Sunday, of course, so we concluded that the day's routine began later than usual. The road by the door was free of traffic; we sat on a wall and watched the high cloud-dappled sky and the bay with its wide scatter of inch and headland.

One car, going westward, and again the empty road. Where, we wondered, was everyone, where was breakfast? Not that we were worried overmuch; it was pleasant to listen to the silence, to see the sheep-dotted fields, a gull balancing on the air-currents, gannets further out above a blue sea, cloud-shadows drifting.

The road still empty. Then a lone cyclist appeared, she also heading west.

'Where are the people of the Inn?'

'Oh!' she replied obviously in some surprise at the question, 'they're gone to Mass.'

'And left the whole house open?'

'Don't worry about that,' she reassured us, 'they'll be back to get you your breakfast,' and she smiled and waved goodbye.

So what was to be done? There was only one answer: we went west the road, as a Kerryman might say, along the winding mountainy way, mountain right, ocean left, a new glimpse of Kerry around every corner, overtook our cyclist friend who smiled and gave us a rather wobbly wave, stopped further on to allow two sheep to cross, and soon afterwards rounded the last sharp bend, and there in front was a new harbour, Ballinskelligs, and on a level rock-strewn place on the seaward side was a small church overflowing with people. As there was no room in the church we joined the many others and sat on rocks outside, said our prayers and admired the view of the great bay that winked at us in the sun-sparkles as much as to say, 'So you thought Derrynane was picturesque?'

And there we stayed until the murmur from the church ended and the crowd began to move and disperse, unhurriedly and with much greeting and gossip. Unhurriedly we also returned to breakfast in the seagull's nest that is the Scarriff Inn, which all that time had been unharmed, as its owners knew it would be.

Could it happen now, in twenty-first century Ireland? Perhaps not, though I want to believe that it could; that the hospitable Inn still perches there and thrives, among the many good kind people that I met whose names I have forgotten. There are others whose names I do remember but whom I will never meet, the great O'Connell, for instance, or his poet Tomás Rua; they are a part of this sea coast, their ghosts still haunt the hills and harbours, and Dan's great house, and the long dunes and the lonely graveyard that twice every day becomes an island, where the poet sleeps, dreaming, it may be, of his precious books. Two hundred years those books have lain on the seabed, yet they are remembered whenever Tomás's song is sung. What learned fishes lurk out there; do they converse in Irish or in English, or do they prefer the Classics? Do the Clouded Yellows still glide in from the south to the autumn lanes? Or might we even now glimpse, through a scud of spray, a Spanish sail in quest of landfall in the twilit harbour? A last question, to which there is no answer: are our memories enriched more by the wild beauty of the place or by the simple honesty and trust that renews our faith in the goodness of the human heart?

Siar Amach

When the call came Davy was ready. In fact he had been ready for the previous fortnight, everything packed. But at Paddy Joe's heart-stirring 'Come soon as you can,' Davy immediately unpacked, went through every item carefully again, and repacked. Twice. Just to be sure. His spare shirt and toothbrush and such were easily seen to, but the two oddly shaped awkward cases (mentally labelled 'Fishing' and 'Music'), were more difficult and required deep thought. Rods, reels, flies, waders, spares for every contingency. Notebooks, pencils. Then the other case, bubble-wrap around the fiddle and bow, spare strings, bridges. It would be disastrous to be caught without essentials that couldn't be had in the villages of the west, though it was true that many places on his itinerary would have a spare fiddle. But he couldn't risk it.

Happier when this was done, he went out to the garden that sloped up from the back of the house and he ambled around among his twenty beehives and his three long rows of raspberries, to see that all was in order and that his bees would be happy until his return. That was his therapy for slowing his heartbeat. Then he poured himself a glass of whiskey and carried it carefully down to the lake-edge. He sat on the log with his back to the old willow, and sipped the liquid gold and listened to the little rest-less waves that stirred the pebbles near his feet, and watched the grey heron that stepped through the shallows on those sensitive claws that could tell the silent movement of a fish from yards away. And whether it was the whiskey or the mild sun of May, or the lilting lullaby of the lake-water, or all three, he presently fell asleep. Indeed, it may not have been any of those; he often fell asleep in the afternoon.

What were his dreams? Very likely much the same as his waking thoughts. The many old friends, loved and outlived. His household, Willie, Moll and the children, who honoured him with affectionate care, though of course it would never do to show them his appreciation of that. His other son, Tom, a good boy too, who would surely come back soon. Or Marge, often it was Marge, but in dreams she was always young, both of them young and full of life and never sad. The background to most of his dreaming was this place, Eadarlocha, Between the Lakes, that in fact was only one lake divided in two almost by the stony ridge called Couss. It was possible to cross there, with care, if you didn't worry about wet feet; local lore said there was no danger as long as the Granny Corriasc, the grey heron, was on guard. This place was part of him, he was part of it, born here, all his life here, the hill rich with wool, the ripples whispering on the pebbles, the heron, grey spirit of the lake, his house and garden, his and Marge's happiness here. Maybe the treasured places he had seen came back. Sceilg Mhichíl, Tara, Ben Bulben, or special pictures came to mind, the Flesk River in spate, 'old pubs where fiddlers love to play', Inch Strand with the Horses of Manannán charging white-maned in from the Atlantic. The less real but no less magical places that he wrote about.

Indeed he had plenty to dream on. Sometimes when he woke, his mind was full of an air or a snatch of a song that continued to annoy him for hours, but on this occasion it was not music but an urgent call, 'You forgot the rosin,' that roused him in confusion. He looked around, found he was still alone, and downing the last of the whiskey, he went back to open the fiddle-case and find that he hadn't forgotten.

Just then the van arrived, with Willie and the others, with questions and banter and advice when he told them his news. 'Don't forget ...'

'Could you not have picked a more awkward day?'

'Did you remember the honey for Paddy Joe?'

'You'll need me to ...'

'Gram, would you have time in Cork to get me some ...?'

Willie drove him to town and helped to stow everything in the train. At Glanmire Station, Paddy Joe was waiting and they set out on the great tour of Cork and Kerry, a fortnight, maybe more, a leisurely journey with many a stop. Their plan was to have no plan, beyond doing their best to leave the city by a different road every time, though always westward, and there was an agreement that if either saw anything of interest, they would stop to investigate. A lane, a hill, a building, some activity whether hurling or a bowl of odds or a row, a sign in Irish which must be scrutinized for errors of spelling or grammar, a friend, a suitable picnic spot, to have an argument, or to study a likely-looking stream. Paddy Joe drove, Davy as navigator guided them (guided is hardly the word, misguided is certainly wrong, if a little nearer the mark), at any rate found for them all sorts of often unexpected and unintended but splendid spots, a ripple over gravel or a shadowed pool, or a little lost public house, a little dark pub with no name at a crossroads with no sign-post, no one there but the man of the house, or, if he happened to be out on the bog or up the hill after the calves, then the woman of the house, and there they would spend hours over a pint or two, or three, in the friendly gloom, and one or other would be reminded of a song, and to have it recalled required that it be sung, or Davy would bring in the fiddle or they would coax a song from the publican or his wife, or they would argue over whether they were going east or west (not that they cared, not that it mattered) or what county they were in, or indeed what world.

They stopped a while in many a town, those wonderful Irish country towns where to an outsider nothing seems to happen from year's end to year's end but where in fact everything happens, Macroom, Bandon, Bantry, Dingle, Listowel. There are equally good towns elsewhere, but Paddy Joe and Davy stayed with the south-west. They understood the importance of keeping in touch with the west, but fishing was the main attraction. Whenever the opportunity arose they dropped a fly on river or stream or lake, asking no one's permission because as far as their thinking went, the waters of Ireland belonged to the people of Ireland, and if sometimes it was illegal (and sometimes it was) it hardly mattered since they seldom caught anything and when they did they threw it back, not for any ethical reason but simply because they had no way of cooking it and besides Paddy Joe didn't care for fish. Up to now they had never made the acquaintance of a water-bailiff.

Old friends were remembered. Larry, born in Durrus, had sat in the same school-desk with Eugene and had poached salmon with him, so now Eugene must be visited, to talk about those ancient times when days were endless and the rivers overflowed with fish. If such visits were reminders of earlier times, of the laughter, the closeness and comradeship, they must also have reminded them of their own mortality, so then to lift their hearts they would sing a verse or two of An Ciarraíoch Mallaithe, The Wicked Kerryman, 'And we will have dancing, music and cheer, Silver and gold, whiskey and beer, Óró for as long as we're here.' Paddy Joe loved that song, written by another O'Sullivan, the great Eoghan Rua.

It would be unthinkable to miss Béal Átha an Ghaorthaidh, where they had met as schoolboys at the Coláiste many years before. There they had learned their Irish and since then had never spoken to each other in English. They knew the place-names there, richer because it was an Irish-speaking area: Drom an Ailthigh, Céim Cora Bhuaile, Tuairín na Lobhar, and then Gúgán, the loveliest place in Ireland, and Coum Rua where the

Lee rises. But Céim an Fhia, *mar a dtéann an fia san oíche*, where the deer goes at night – what a perfect name for a mountain pass: The Deer's Step. A great song had to be sung there, a song about a battle long ago, 'The mountain shook with the sound of arms.'

From here they looked down on the western mountains. Loch na mBreac Dearg, hidden away in the hills, was discussed, as always. It was unlikely, they agreed, that it held any trout; that had been accepted more than once before. And yet – there was the nagging thought: why the name Lake of the Red Trout? 'Maybe we should investigate?' Every year, summer after summer the same tentative suggestion, never acted on. It may be that in their wisdom they knew it was as well not to know for sure one way or the other. Better by far the magic of the name and the disturbing delight of possibility.

Their expeditions were not entirely aimless, but had a serious side. Not too serious. They collected music and they collected places, places and their names. In their radio series a few years earlier, they emphasized the poetic richness of Irish place-names, the most striking of them being in rural places, often mountainous and thinly populated, where the names were less anglicized and corrupted. Their choice of examples was wide: Glendalough, Cushendall, Gweedore, Dromahair, some for their music, some for their associations, their legends, their mystery. Sliabh Bloom, Dún na Séad, Cooley, Cashel of the Kings, Classie-bawn, Clonmacnoise. They gave translations where possible, and suggested that dwelling-houses should be given names based on place-names.

They were working now in a vague way towards a book of songs in Irish with their music. Both loved the great slow airs and argued about which was the greatest. Paddy Joe said Cailín na Gruaige Doinne 'for its perfection of words as well as music', Davy suggested The Coolun, or Carrickfergus, or maybe Tiarna Mhuigheo – but how could anyone decide?

Their different acquaintance with machinery made for arguments, too. Davy owned a watch and a bicycle, and could, but seldom did, use a telephone. Paddy Joe had lived all his adult life in the city where he had lectured in the University, and was accepted therefore as the expert on all mechanical things, from the wheelbarrow to the internet. His contribution to their tour included his car, a recording machine and a marvellous device called a volcano kettle – basically two metal cylinders one inside the other, which, when the space between the cylinders was filled with water, and a bundled-up copy of the *Examiner* was ignited in the inner cylinder, would provide boiling water in five minutes.

On through Kerry, west and west again, siar amach, Anascaul, Dingle, Coumenole, Brandon. They sat on the Atlantic's rim where the waves broke in thunder on the stacks and in the sea-caves. Oonagloor came to mind, The Cave of the Pigeons, which Paddy Joe claimed for Cork, but Davy said no, it was on the Waterford coast. They watched the gannets, their power and grace, and the red-beaked aerobats of the sea-margins, motionless a while as they leaned on the updrafts, then letting go, turning away to sweep downwind, and with a chuckle to slide smoothly over the cliff-edge. Sitting on a breezy headland the two old voyagers brewed their tea and ate their sandwiches, looked out through the blue air to the Blaskets, Isles of the Blest, Scarriff, the Skelligs, dark shapes on the horizon where the sun went down.

The companions were alike in their invincible optimism, their refusal of defeat, yet differed on many subjects and argued amicably about most. Did Glenanaar exist in fact or only in fiction? What place came oftenest to mind? Adrigole, Tooraneena, Corcomroe, Garryowen, Lyreanearla, Glenasmole? Did some vowel-sounds stick in the memory more than others?

Every day brought new delights to these old hearts. They drank old whiskey, they sang old songs, their thoughts dwelt on the magic places, they spoke of yesterdays, and they felt sorry for the young who had no such happiness. But they were not old. Many who didn't know Davy but who had seen him sitting quietly by the lake, probably thought of him as a man whose time was over, maybe just waiting for the Man Above to call him. But Davy had never grown old and he was far more likely to have been waiting for a call from the man below in Cork.

Reluctantly they turned east. Instinct, or luck, brought them to where there was good music; they were known and welcomed. Sliabh Luachra was an essential stop, and on this occasion it once again provided a night of music and song, exhilaration, joy, comradeship, laughter, exaltation, satisfied longing, *mórtas cine*.

And as is the way of things, after that triumphant night, the very next day disaster struck, in the person of an officious water-bailiff. A grassy boreen had lured them to where a mountain stream came tumbling down, with scattered boulders, sudden pools, ledges and gravel bars. They gazed in admiration and Davy quoted, 'Where stone is dark under froth.' It was a challenge, an invitation, a trap. They were summoned to court. But if the owner of the fishing-rights thought that these old fellows were an easy mark he had made a serious error of judgement. No doubt deep in some musty vault a crumbling parchment with a broken seal states that 10,000 plantation acres are thereby legally transferred to Hollow Blades of the City of London, in recognition of financial aid for the Army of the Commonwealth in the prosecution of its war against the Irish enemy; by the time Paddy Joe and Davy fell foul of this bit of legal larceny, the land had been grudgingly returned to the Irish enemy, but all the rivers had flowed into the pocket of one Timothy Shepton. All this was smoothly explained by complainant's legal team. Defendants, however, demanded to see documentary proof that the rights were as stated, and, without benefit of legal representation, argued that they had not broken the law because no document could be produced which forbade fishing but only 'the taking of fish', and they had taken no fish. That this had been a huge disappointment to them at the time was not mentioned in court.

As luck happened, the case was heard before Justice Tackaberry, a noted fisherman. Now it would be astonishing if Tom Tackaberry had never in a long lifetime dropped a Greenwell's Glory on a forbidden pool, but whatever about that, he looked down thoughtfully over his glasses at the two miscreants and no one knows what memories disturbed the cool logic of his mind. Did a line of Yeats occur to him, 'Bald heads forgetful of their sins'? He spoke with his usual clarity and decisiveness, 'Probation act!' or some such legal phrase, and to the Clerk, 'These gentlemen

will put £5 in the Court Box as they go out,' and they thanked
the Court and left, and went on a week's batter. The local Garda
Sergeant, Jarlath Coen, kept an eye on them, made sure they got
into no mischief, and towards the end of the week suggested that
they might like to consider taking the pledge, or perhaps head
for home, avoiding licensed premises if at all possible.

So it was a big bunch of flowers and a box of chocs for
Tilly, the sergeant's wife, but serious thought had to be given
to a suitable gift for the sergeant; they consulted their friend
Markey Kerr, who by devious ways procured a bottle of liquor,
made by a small private distiller in an abandoned turf-cutting out
beyond Purth. The bottle being unlabelled, Paddy Joe manufac-
tured a very nice label with curlicues around the edge, on which
they wrote 'For internal use only', then wrapped the bottle and
delivered it with the flowers and sweets to Coen's. Mrs Coen
wanted them right or wrong to come in for a cup of tea, but they
explained (the shameless liars), that they always had to be home
before dark, and so they couldn't delay. They said their good-
byes and were well away from the sergeant's jurisdiction before
he came off duty.

Their journey home from Kenmare after their day in court
and their week in the jigs took in Sherkin and Cape Clear,
more names to be added to their mental store of fabulous
places. Trebizond and Samarkand meant less to them than
Aghadoe and Glenflesk, Tomies and Purple Mountain. They
sang of those magic places as though they were drunk on the

names and the music of the names and on nothing more. For ten days after his return from the far west, Davy moved in a dream. Of Glandore and Rosscarbery. Of Mount Gabriel, with its suggestion of angels hovering over Goleen. And he loved Crookhaven. But he loved Eadarlocha too, and when he had settled down again he was perfectly content, happy in his round of self-imposed duties until the west beckoned again.

He spent a morning tying in his raspberry canes. Then Moll called him, and they ate their midday meal together. Moll went back to her bread, it was her day for baking, and he finished in the garden. Tired then, he carried his glass of whiskey down to the seat by the lake. He was glad to sit in the pleasant shade of the willow; it had been a long morning's work and his back ached, though he felt a quiet sense of achievement, too. He looked across the lake towards the hill, where there were sixteen lambs, big and sturdy enough now to be safe from predators. Later in the day, he would help the two grandchildren with their homework, though he struggled with changed ideas about maths, and they laughed and tried to explain to him. He always enjoyed that. He must not, however, let them see how proud he was of them. All his family were well. He had no news of Tom, but surely there would be a letter soon.

Eighty-seven years, a long road with many turns, that had always led him back to Eadarlocha, where it began. And Marge — how many years now? Tomorrow he must bring her some flowers. A big armful of lilac. She loved lilac; it was she who had planted it. How strange that the green bough should still live and thrive. Tomorrow then. The sunlight across the lake was reflected from the ripples so that light and shade danced all around him. The heron, their grey guardian, patrolled the lake-shore. All was well. He leaned back against the fissured bole and drifted into sleep.

Growing Up

He drifted into the yard, where Mam was feeding the hens, and asked for a bit of bread, 'a stale bit will do, ma'am, and maybe a small drop of milk, and God bless you.' Mam sized him up with one shrewd glance and said, 'Go up there and sit on the chair by the kitchen door. I'll talk to you in a minute.' Then she looked around for me. I had slipped into the stable to avoid being given a job to do, even though I was curious about the stranger and wanted to know what was going to happen. But of course Mam knew where I was, Mam knew everything. 'Tom, come out here and look after the hens,' and then headed for the kitchen. The teapot sizzled as usual at the edge of the fire, so our travelling man got a mug of scalding hot tea with plenty of sugar and milk, and both brown bread and white soda with currants in it, and plenty of butter. 'He looks hungry,' Mam said to Aunt Kate and it was Aunt Kate who did the catering while Mam went to talk to him. I heard her asking about his family but he didn't make her any the wiser.

He was vague about his name — as indeed about most things, especially anything to do with himself — and somehow he finally became known as Rich. It was a name, not a description. Where had he come from? Why? What had he worked at? Had he a wife, a family? We found few answers to these natural questions. The one thing that was not vague about him, as we soon learned, was his love and knowledge of horses, and so it seemed most appropriate that he eventually wound up sleeping in the loft above the stable, where a straw mattress and the proximity of the two big plough-horses helped to provide him with some small comfort.

Naturally, Daddy had to be consulted about this when he came back from the fields. What was to be done about the new-comer? I suppose I knew even then, the way children know such things without being told, that the matter had already been decided, but Daddy had to be asked for his opinion; the conventions had to be observed.

The wanderer showed no inclination to leave, but behaved, with a gentle insistence, as though he thought this was where he was destined to be. He admired the house, and the seat in the sun by the back door, and the cows, and he smiled at the members of the family as they passed into and out of the house. 'Poor soul,' said Mam, 'he looks lost.' Even Aunt Kate took to him and it was she who suggested the loft over the stable.

John and I became his special friends. Ned usually trailed along after us, but he was my younger brother, only five, and wasn't important. John, who was four years older than me, wasn't very strong but he was clever and had ideas and was good at finding and making things. 'We'll make a bed for Rich,' he said.

'But he has a bed.' 'Not a real bed.' So we got some boards from the floor of the other loft, the far end that was never used and where some of the boards were loose, and we made a kind of big box that we filled with straw. We put it against the warm chimney of the boiler-house, well away from the little window in the gable. Later on we found an old sack to keep the east wind from blowing in that window at night. There was a ragged cobwebby coat hanging on a nail in the car-shed. 'Nobody wants it. We'll make a pillow with it.' Next, the stairs, not much better than a ladder really, that led to Rich's loft, because Rich was sometimes a bit unsteady. It was John who thought of using an old discarded harrow that he found half-buried in the corner of the haggard. We needed a good strong pole to support the stairs, so we set off down across the Big Field and across to the far side of the stream in Mullenreagh and after a bit of a search we found a young ash tree and cut it down. We used a bill-hook; we weren't supposed to use it, maybe because it could be dangerous or because we might take the edge off, and we didn't let Ned or Rich use it. With the pole and the harrow and some good bits of the ladder we made a staircase that we were very proud of.

Rich did his best to help around the place, cutting sticks for the fire, or bringing water from the well. He sometimes scuffled the gravel in Aunt Kate's garden, but she couldn't trust him to do any weeding. 'He doesn't know a flower from a weed,' she would say indignantly. He was willing to do any errand, to go to the shop in the street where one of the three houses had a shop which sold a few basic things, matches, candles, sweets, tea and sugar, or to the post office. In our house, of course, there was no scarcity of messengers unless it was in school-time so it usually meant that Rich and one or two of us went, and on the way, or on the way back, there would be adventures – tadpoles, or chestnuts in the autumn, or hiding in the tree near the school and watching who went by, or being chased by Cullimore's wicked dog, or building a dam on Whelan's stream to make the water run across the field. He didn't as a rule play a very active part, but took an interest and made suggestions, or acted as a look-out (he was a very good whistler) and he could be depended on completely if there were secrets to be kept. Although Mam always told us not to delay, we'd often stop a while at the cross. We'd sit on the three big flat stones at the corner and watch who went by, on foot or on carts; there would often be young fellows just hanging around, or maybe wrestling or arguing, boasting, playing marbles. I remember how smooth and shiny those three stones were and I realize now why they were like that: it was because they had been polished by the trouser-seats of the many spectators who had used them as grandstand during pitch-and-toss schools, or a bit of hurling or football, or in earlier times, dances. After Mass on fine Sundays, you could sit there to talk, or smoke your pipe – there would always be someone there. It was a meeting-place; Rich said it was the centre of the parish. I never saw dancing there; at the time I'm thinking of, dances were held in people's houses or barns.

Once in a while, a policeman would cycle out from town but he could be seen coming along the straight stretch of road, and there was plenty of time for the pitch-and-toss players to scatter, usually up through the graveyard, past the chapel and the school to the mountain road. On one occasion that was long remembered, he outflanked the gamblers by cycling up the mountain road and coming down on them *aniar adtuaidh*. Most of them escaped through Lizzie Kinsella's garden, but he captured two, gave them a severe lecture, and worst of all confiscated a penny from each of them. As he was about to re-mount his bicycle, however, he stopped and called them back, handed back their money and said, 'You're to put those in the priest's box on Sunday. Do you hear me now! Without fail! I'll be talking to Fr Doyle about it.'

That had happened before Rich came into our lives, and when we told him about it, he surprised us when he said, 'Served them right!'

'Why, Rich? People always played pitch-and-toss there.'

'Because it's illegal.'

'But why?'

'It's an insult to the queen's image,' and when he saw that we didn't understand, he said, 'Don't you know the queen's head is on every coin?' I suppose maybe we did know that; anyway as none of us had a coin to demonstrate what Rich was telling us, he put two fingers into one of his waistcoat pockets, took out a small string-bag, opened it carefully and shook out into his palm some tiny silver coins. He wouldn't let us handle them but let us look at them closely; we had seen threepenny bits before, of course, but there were also tiny silver pennies and two-penny pieces. 'Look at the queen's head,' and then put them with great care back in the bag, tightened the cord and stowed it again in his pocket.

'Why did you never spend them, Rich?' He looked a bit shocked. 'Oh no, I couldn't spend those. They were a present from Mrs Bannerman. She was a lovely lady. She said they were a thank you for bringing the family to so many lovely places and bringing them safe home again. And that was only a year before she died. And she was young. Her husband went off to his house in England after that and never came back to Ireland. Her little baby died the same time and they were buried together in the one grave.'

I wanted to ask him if those were really silver buttons on his waistcoat, and were they a uniform, and if they were, was it because he was a coachman, but just then he stood up, and said something about seeing to the horses and walked away from us. This was more information than we'd ever got, up to then, about Rich's former life. We surmised that that might have been when Rich lost his job as coachman.

John said, 'I think he's sad talking about Mrs Bannerman and the baby.'

My only sister near my age was Kitty, who was only two years older than me. Sometimes we went for walks, maybe to paddle in the stream that came down from the mountain. It had places where the water was green and sliding, and little waterfalls with froth, and pebbly stretches, or dark pools under the hazel boughs where the river stopped to rest. We looked for fish and found none, and frogs, and floated stick-boats in the water, and she would bring home flowers that she put in a jam-jar but they were always drooping and wilted by the next morning. She was a quiet girl, with red hair, and she never fell out with me. She was my favourite sister. Those times when we went rambling were special,

we didn't want any of the others to know, although I think now
that they probably did know; everyone knew that our two were
special friends. Our favourite place was down through the Grove,
and out the tall iron gate into the stony lane that joined our farm
to the outlying land. We knew that it had once been the main
road between Wexford and Ross, so it had been wide and well-
paved, though now the *sceachs* and briars and blackthorns made it
narrower. We loved especially to walk there in summer time, sheltered from every breeze in the deep lanes that were drowsy with
bees and flowers. There was a wild plant that we picked because
its spiky yellow flowers smelt of lemons. There were things to eat,
sorrel, sloes, blackberries and hazelnuts, depending on the time
of year. A quarter of a mile on, we took the right-hand branch
into our fields; and always we went to the empty house where
we knew Mam and Aunt Kate had been born and spent the first
years of their lives until the family moved to our present house.
Another family had taken their place; the last member of that
family married, the wedding party went on for a week until every
scrap of food and drink was gone, and every song had been sung,
and then the dancing had to stop, they turned the key in the door
and went to America, leaving the empty house to fall into ruin.
We always went to the doorway and looked in, but we were a bit
scared of it and of the jackdaws that flew up from the chimney
and talked and squabbled. Fascinated, we had to go to see it, but
frightened too, and usually very quiet as we went away.

My first journey along that lane between the tall hawthorns
was on horseback, when I was only four or five years old. Phil,
my eldest brother, was working in our farthest field; it must have

been in late autumn, but as the day was dry and sunny, he brought me along, too. He threw me up on Dick's broad back, where I hung on to his mane as I was told to do. I wasn't nervous; in fact, I enjoyed that warm seat, high above the ground among boughs and bees and birds, swaying to the big horse's powerful steps. I had a busy day. I stalked fierce wild animals, tigers mostly; I shot an elephant that was hiding in the bushes, right between the eyes I got him, and he fell down stone dead at my feet; I raced up and down the newly-cut furrows until Phil called me and told me to collect scribs for the fire. When the Angelus rang the two of us made a camp-fire between two big stones and boiled water for the tea. I got my bottle of milk from the stream where I had left it to keep it cool, and then I sat beside my big brother and we ate our sandwiches, and he drank tea and I had milk. We sat on his old coat with our backs to the ditch; I warned him about the tigers, and he said he'd keep a sharp lookout; I offered to shoot them all, but he said no, he thought we'd be pretty safe as long as we kept the fire going. I asked him if the crockodoyles had anything to do with the Doyles who lived in the street, but he didn't think so. I had to eat just bread and butter because the pismires had got into the little bag of sugar.

After that he went back to his work, I got more dry twigs for the fire, and then I went exploring in the jungle at the far edge of the field. The jungle was dangerous, it was full of rattlesnakes and monkeys and when I crossed the stream I went cautiously by the stepping-stones because you have to be very careful where there are crockodoyles and sharks. Of course I had my gun, but it wasn't easy, I can tell you. Then I had to run back to put more scribs on the fire. Phil stopped at the headland. 'I have a job for you,' he said, 'an important job. I want you to sit here near the fire and watch out for tigers and things. I don't think there's many around, but keep your gun loaded just in case.' Sitting there at the top corner I could see the whole field where it sloped down towards the river, and also the edge of the jungle, so I loaded my gun and began to watch, but I must have fallen asleep, because the next thing I remember, Phil was calling me to tell me it was time to go home. When he put me up on the horse's back he said, 'Don't let him go down to the river. He'll want to go down, to drink. Don't let him.' That was all very well, but when we came to where the path branched, Dick turned left, and what could I do to stop him? How could I be expected to turn the huge shoulders that could haul great loads of hay and corn, or his big battering hooves that knocked sparks out of the stones? I heard, 'Keep him up … didn't I tell you … ' but he might as well have asked me to stop the sun in the sky, Dick kept going and then lowered his head to drink while I tried desperately to keep myself from sliding down the horse's big smooth neck, and Phil started to laugh and I knew he was laughing at me. Well, I managed to hold on and didn't fall into the water, Dick had a good drink, Phil had a good laugh, and I have never forgotten that day.

Rich became one of our household, accepted, expected, depended on. Some of our neighbours must have wondered at Mam taking in this stray – I heard Tim's mother saying one time, 'Hasn't she enough to do with that houseful, without takin' in another. And a stranger, no kith or kin' – but Mam didn't think like that. If she stopped to think about it at all she probably thought, 'Well, there's fifteen in this house. One more won't make much difference.' Once I heard Tim's mother saying that Mam took in Rich to fill the gaps in her life that her dead children had left. Another John – there were two Johns in our family, he was the second oldest boy – died the same year as Teresa who died as an infant, and Mam's mother, our Granny Cowman, died the year after, so it was very sad for Mam, even though she still had a big family. I never knew John or Teresa, and so I never missed them.

Rich hadn't the skill or the strength for farm work, knew nothing about it which was strange until we found that he never had worked on a farm and that his gifts really were in his dealings with the two plough-horses and the pony. Never had they been better cared for, never had they looked so well; he would happily spend hours brushing and grooming them, talking quietly, whether to himself or to the horses we couldn't tell, or whistling tunelessly; never had they been so petted and loved. He had a few other jobs too, the most important one being to make sure all the fowl were safe at nightfall, in case the fox was on the prowl. In the coldest of winter he carried his mattress down and put it in the centre stall in the stable, the horses in the outer stalls, plenty of straw and hay, a blanket that Aunt Kate had found for him and patched, an old cast-off overcoat of Daddy's. If he couldn't sleep he talked to the horses. 'No, it doesn't disturb them. When they're asleep they don't hear me and if they're awake they always agree with me.'

We were able to show him how to make a *cléibhín*: you prop up a riddle with a forked stick, tie a long string to the stick, put some meal or bread crumbs under the riddle and then hide somewhere with the other end of the string and wait for a hungry finch to fly down. We often gave up because we got impatient. He said we shouldn't shoot at birds with our catapults, but maybe it was alright to catch them and keep them in a cage, if we were kind to them. He fed them even when we forgot sometimes. We had found the big bird-cage in the loft, cleaned it up a bit, straightened the bent part and did some repairs with hairpins that we got on the table in Aunt Kate's room while she was out milking the cows. In any case, although we used our catapults to shoot at crows or magpies, I remember only once killing a bird, and that was a small brown bird that I shot at without really expecting to hit it. I was more embarrassed than elated, almost ashamed when I picked up the small limp body, still warm.

Frocken Sunday was when we went to the mountain. I can't remember if the frockens were put to any practical use, so maybe they were only an excuse for a day out. It was mostly the older people who picked them. The younger ones played games, and there was great fun and teasing, and we met all our friends, and we brought picnics, and it was late when we got home, hot and tanned and dusty, and we could see the silent shadows of the leatherwing bats against the sky. Tim and I always went together those days; he was my friend. He was my cousin, too, we were the same age and in the same class, but I was much bigger than he was. Our uncle Johnny, the one who had the shop in town, never missed that big day. He said he wasn't going to break a good habit – he had been picking frockens since he was three. Then he came home with us after the mountain and we knew he'd bring shop-bread and sticky buns with currants, and he'd have his annual tea with us. He lined us up then according to height, all the younger ones, and said, 'You're after gettin' as *tall*. . .', and gave each of us a sixpence. We'd race off then to the dairy and measure all our heights on the door-jamb and sure enough we *had* got taller. There must have been mountain days when the sun didn't shine, but somehow I don't remember them.

Indeed there must have been many wet days but we went out anyway. We put on our caps and boots and mostly paid little attention to the rain. There was no show-off about that – outside was our natural place. Up early always, school-days or holidays, and then out. We slept in the house and ate there, but outside was where we lived. On very wet days, if the hay wasn't in, we could play marbles in the hay-barn, or football if there was room, or we might be told by Daddy to clean out the stable or one of the calf-houses. John wasn't allowed out in the rain though, because he might catch cold which would be very bad for him. We made things, toys and gadgets, in the car-shed, out of bits of iron or timber or whatever we could find. Anyone who had a penknife sharpened it on the stone, and carved things. But even on really cold wet days we could make ourselves cosy in the hay and listen to Rich talking, mostly about horses. He told us about the coach-horses he used to drive for the Bannermans. That was a part of his life that he did sometimes talk about. The coach-horses had magic names, Prince and Beauty, Black Bob and Blazer, and there was a coach and four. The Bannermans were big people, with a house in England as well as in Ireland. But they were Irish, too, because one of the Bannermans had married an O'Moore lady, and he told us about the banshee that cried about the woods or on the turrets of the big house when one of the family was going to die. 'The banshee follows the O'Moores,' he told us. After that, any time I heard the voice of the snipe, like a goat in the April twilight, I pretended it was the banshee. I half-believed it, and always hurried home. The marshy land by the stream at the bottom of Knockahoon hill was where the snipe lived and where the dusk smelled of garlic in April. And wasn't it a funny thing that garlic is what keeps you safe from banshees and other bad things like that, so Rich told us. He told us about the forty eight horses, the coach-horses that he loved best of all, hunters too, work-horses and ponies. They were polo ponies, and he explained how polo was played. I think we hardly believed him, yet if Rich said so, it must be true. There were fifty rooms in the big house and a hundred windows. But we were able to tell him that our house used to be called Cromwell Cottage for the reason that Cromwell slept there the night before he attacked Wexford town. It was John who found out about the name of the house; our family never used that name, but it was on old maps, and Lar, the blacksmith, told us it was quite true that Cromwell had stayed there. We were proud that he had chosen our house, but a bit doubtful about Cromwell himself; he hadn't a very good reputation and was said to have sacked Wexford. Ned said, 'I bet he went to see Uncle Johnny, on account of being at our house the night before.' The others laughed, but I remember that I was wondering if he had sacked Uncle Johnny's shop too — and how exactly do you sack a place, anyway? Our grasp of history wasn't very sound. We also boasted to Rich that our house was where the landlord lived before he went to live in one of his other houses, and that he had made big changes, for instance what we called the front door had once opened into the farmyard, but he put the farmyard around at the back and made a new back-door in the kitchen, and then he built all the stone and slated out-houses. He put big windows and a double door in the front wall and a curved drive out to the road. And we emphasised to Rich that an *Architect* had been employed to see to all those changes. We thought he would be impressed to hear that, but he paid little heed to it and we were disappointed. It was very hard to interest him in other things, apart from horses.

We had many adventures, Kitty and I, and one of our best places was to go down the road to the bottom of the hill, where our road joined the New Road, and then we went up the steps at the far side. They were very steep and there were thirty two, we counted them. Then, out of breath, we would lie on the grass where the land levelled out at the top, and when we got our breath back, we went to the pool with the bulrushes that we regarded as our pool, to watch the dragon-flies, and once we frightened a snipe that flew away in zig-zags, but we saw it clearly, and although I had often heard the snipe calling, it was the first time I had seen one. Then along the lane and after a drink from the holy well we'd cross the field to the old graveyard where many of Mam's family are buried, including her mother. We went there every Pattern Day, and once when we were standing by our Granny's grave, Mam told us, 'One day I'll be buried here,' but of course we didn't believe her, we thought she was joking. Another time we turned off the lane before we reached the well and went to the walled garden of the Big House. The gate was open and we peeped in but just then a man we didn't know came along behind us; we thought he would be angry but he set down his wheelbarrow and looked at us and even though he had fierce-looking whiskers and was very tall, he spoke kindly. 'What's your name, lassie? And your brother?' (but he said brither). 'Where do you live?' and when Kitty answered him he asked us if we would like some strawberries. He had a funny way of speaking but Kitty said, 'Yes, please,' so we went with him to a small shed, very dark, that smelled of clay, and he poked on a shelf and found an empty sugar-bag. He filled it with strawberries, there were plenty of them growing in a sunny place with straw around them and a big high wall behind. Then he said, 'Give those to your mother,' but he said mither, and Kitty said, 'Thanks, sir' and off we went.

As we were going back down the steep steps, I said, 'Give those to your mither,' and we started to laugh. Kitty stumbled and spilled the strawberries and they rolled down the steps and into the bushes. We tried to find them but most of them were lost, and then Kitty started to cry, so I said, 'We'll go back and ask for more. There's plenty,' but Kitty didn't want to do that. She came with me as far as the garden gate but wouldn't go in. So I went in and found the gardener and told him what had happened and could we have some more.

He looked hard at me. 'Where's your sister?'

'At the gate, sir.'

He marched me to the gate, but when he saw Kitty he could see she had been crying. 'All right. Just this once. And be more careful this time, and don't let me see you here ever again,' and then as we were going away with our second lot of strawberries he said after us, 'Not for a month, anyway,' and he gave a kind of growl that sounded as if he was laughing. After that we always tried to make sure that a month went by before we visited the Big House garden again. Mam told us his name was Mr Smith and that he was from Scotland, and if we saw him again we were to say thanks very much for the strawberries. Whenever I wanted to make Kitty laugh I only had to say, 'Gie those to yer mither,' and she would say, 'You mustn't make fun of him. He's a nice man,' but she would laugh all the same.

We hadn't many visitors. The postman came now and again on his bicycle. A few women from the cottages nearby came for milk. Then there were our regular callers, mostly members of farm families and usually relations of ours, who paid their customary visits on Sundays between the Masses, or on Saturday nights to sit around the big fire and talk or play cards. The tinkers could be depended on to call maybe once or twice a year and there would be milk-cans and tea-drawers for them to mend; or the thatcher might be needed; and once when a wheel had to be replaced on one of the common cars, a wheelwright arrived, and we became experts on that trade and showed off in school with our new knowledge: oak for the box, ash for the spokes, elm for the felloes. We specially liked that word felloes, John in particular loved collecting words, the bigger the better.

When I think of hay-making, the sun is blazing down and we are sitting in the shade of a hay-cock drinking bottles of milk and eating brown bread and butter with sugar on it. We helped with the hay, too, or thought we were helping, and when I got older I learned how to make a hay-cock. Hay-making was great fun when the weather was good, but heart-breaking for

Daddy and the others when it was wet. Later in the year, at the corn, all the boys in their turn, and some of my sisters too, learned how to tie a sheaf or to make stooks. Our corn was ground at the mill, half a mile or so down the road. We liked going there. However, the busiest, most exciting day of the year was threshing day: the noisy smoking engine could be seen and heard while it was still far away on the top road and when it turned in our gate it never failed to knock one of the capstones off the piers. There was so much help from all the neighbours that we weren't needed, more likely to be in the way than to be asked to help, and although we loved the novelty and excitement, we were told to keep away from the centre of activity because it was dangerous. We hung around with Bob and Brownie and tried to get them to catch the mice that ran out of the ricks, but the dogs were useless, the cats were much better. Thinking back now, the picture I recall most clearly is of one October when the ricks of corn weren't finished and covered until after dark. Rich called us, Kitty, Ned and me, and asked if we'd like to see the Hunter's Moon. We had never heard of it before, so of course we went with him, not sure what to expect. The sky was clear; there wasn't a breath of wind. He brought us to the corn-ricks in the haggard and pointed to the gap between the two huge ricks, the gap where the threshing engine would be on the following day. The side of one rick was black dark, the other was bright and clear, and out beyond, watching us from the unclouded sky was a great yellow bowl of creamy moon, smiling and calm. Rich said, 'That's the Hunter's Moon,' though there was no need to tell us. Kitty put her arms around me and Ned, and we gazed at it in a breathless silence. Sometimes I think I can still see the three small children standing in the moonlight between the towering ricks and gazing at the biggest roundest yellowest moon that ever was. There's no accounting for what memory will hold on to, or what it will discard.

The years went by, and I grew taller, and so did John and Frances and Kitty and Ned. Everyone else seemed to stay the same. Rich, anyway, didn't change: Daddy tried to get him to whitewash the house and the lawn-piers, but he wasn't good at it, and splashed the whitewash onto the windows and the sills. He had that one great gift, he could talk to horses. I think Daddy was a bit cross with him, but he was never cross for long, and Mam said, 'Everybody has one gift, and you can't expect more.' The upshot of it was that it was left like that: anything to do with horses or transport, but little else, was Rich's business.

Kitty went away to learn cookery and house-keeping and things like that, and John went to college in Ross. All the boys in our family went in turn to the Christian Brothers school in Wexford when we finished in our own school, but John was a boarder in Ross, he wouldn't be able to travel in and out to Wexford, especially in the winter. Years afterwards he confided to me that he had been desperately lonely when he went to college, and missed his parents and all his sisters and brothers, and Rich too, and that his reading and the new things he was learning helped him to forget his loneliness; he tried to explain also that the first time he came home on holidays he wanted to get back to the way things had always been, but couldn't get over how different the farm was and even his family, but later he realised that they hadn't changed, but it was he who was different, seeing people and things in a different way. Rich was the only one who was the same. And Mam and Daddy of course. Even after Kitty came home again, she and I didn't go walking together so much, but I loved her just the same. She was tall and had long red hair that she coiled up in a bun. We hurled or played football in the field at the front of the house, me and Ned mostly, and some-times some of our older brothers. Rich would come to watch and when I played well I hoped he would praise me but he never did, and I was disappointed. He knew nothing about hurling, anyway, it wasn't played in his part of the country. When we asked where that was, all he would say was, 'The midlands.'

John finished in the college in 1901. I remember that date well because it was the year Frances died. She was only seventeen, a pale quiet girl who seldom came out to join in our games, but helped Aunt Kate in the house. She didn't talk much, ever, but at times she would surprise you with a sudden shy smile that lighted up her face and that vanished again as quickly as it came. I can't explain how I felt when she died, why I didn't grieve more. Maybe boys of that age – I was twelve – are too wrapped up in their own concerns, a kind of indifference to others, a selfishness, or are they not sensitive enough, or is it that they have no expe-rience of grief, or don't know how to express it or deal with it? I was more confused than sad. Our house was full of weeping. One day I came on Mamie and Jo with their arms around each other, crying, not saying anything, just crying. What I remember most is how small and still and white she looked in the big bed where she was waked. Someone had brought white roses, I remember that. And the candles, and the way their flames jumped when someone knelt down to say a prayer at her bed. Now I watched the grave still face on the pillow, the face that was, and was not, my sister; I knew that that face would never again light up with her little fugitive smile. 'Where is she gone?' I whispered to Kitty. 'Where is she now?' 'She's gone to heaven,' Kitty assured me and I knew she was right, and the funny thought came that it's much worse for the ones who are left than for the one who has died, who feels no pain, no worry or anxiety or regret or sadness. It was my first encounter with the great mystery. There was a queer empty feeling about the house after she was gone, and a silence. I think Rich liked Frances best of all: he wouldn't go to her funeral, but sulked and gloomed for a long time afterwards, and then he took to going to the grave and sitting there for ages, just thinking or saying his prayers or maybe telling her he was sorry for not being at her funeral.

When the County Councils were set up, sometime in the nineties, Daddy got a position as a land-valuer, which meant he would be called for advice now and again and might have to travel to different parts of the county. This work brought in a bit of extra money, but there was never any to spare; although our farm was fairly big, it was not good land, and there was such a big number of us depending on it. So in 1903, one of my oldest brothers, Pat, was sent to New York, where Uncle Tom, who lived there, would help him to get a job. It was a very exciting time with all the preparations for his journey. When he was gone, however, the house was very quiet, and Mam hardly said a word and the girls were quiet too, but it took a while for me to understand that Pat was gone and we would never see him again, it was like as if he had died. I was sorry then for being cross with him about the penknife, because you see, he got a new penknife from Uncle Johnny before he left, and he gave his old one to Ned, and I had expected to get it, but now I was sorry for being cross and it was too late to tell him.

The corn was always brought to Cullen's mill to be ground. I often went there and I knew it well. Especially I remember the last time Rich and I went. He and I set off, down the hill, along the New Road to the old Enniscorthy road and so down the leafy lane till we reached the mill, shady under the trees. Rich, as he always did, sat up very straight and held the reins high as I suppose he had held them when he drove the Bannerman horses. When the meal was ready and loaded, Rich handed me the reins. I was delighted. I was well able to manage our horses – I was sixteen then – but Rich had never before allowed me to drive if he was with me. So I held the reins high, like him, and said, 'Ho, hup there, Dick,' in imitation. (Dick was very old by then, but still as sound and reliable as ever).

I hoped Rich would praise my driving, but he didn't; in fact I remember now that he was very quiet on the way home, though I didn't notice at the time. When we got home, we lifted out the sacks together and I helped him to unyoke the horse. But as he and I lifted the heavy collar up onto the wooden peg on the stable wall, he stumbled, fell against the wall and to my consternation slid slowly down till he lay in a funny shape on the straw and cobbles.

I ran to the house and Mam came back with me. 'Get Jim and Phil. They're in the haybarn.' When the three of us got back, Mam and Aunt Kate had put Rich sitting against the stable wall and he had come to. He insisted he was better and asked to be carried up to his bed over the stable. Aunt Kate prepared hot milk and goody and I was told to look out for him and make sure he was alright and to get him anything he wanted. He didn't complain, but he seemed very weak and all the fight had gone out of him. The priest came to see him, and afterwards he conferred with Mam and Daddy and I heard some of what he said: 'He's very weak and resigned … it's as if he knew … he's all prepared to go anyway … maybe the doctor … but I don't know … said I was to thank you for … he was very anxious that I'd tell you that.' I didn't like hearing them talk like that, I didn't want to believe he was very sick.

In ones and twos we went to see him. He smiled and shook hands with everyone, and thanked us over and over, and in an old-fashioned way he kissed Mam's and Aunt Kate's hands. I couldn't believe but that he would be well in a day or two. No matter what I was doing, I remembered to go to see if he needed anything; I'd go to the middle rung of the stairs and from there I could see his bed, and if he was asleep I didn't disturb him. Aunt Kate made hot drinks for him, and food that she thought he might like, but he ate very little. When I did speak to him, he took my hand, and spoke about 'all the adventures'. His voice was weak and he stopped often as if to get his breath.

Late on the day after the priest's visit, I went to check on him as usual. I went half-way up the stairs and looked across at his bed. He seemed to be sleeping, but as I watched he suddenly sat up very straight, held up his two hands in that way he had of holding the reins and said in a loud clear voice, 'Ho, hup there! Pick 'em up, boy! Hup, you beauty!' and shook the reins and flicked his long whip, and then fell back on his pillow, and I knew he was dead. Don't ask me how, but I knew. And even stranger than that, I wasn't afraid, though I had never before seen anyone die. I wasn't afraid because he looked so happy, as if his last journey had brought him to a place of shining peace.

It was in September that same year that Daddy got a bad wetting on his way home from Enniscorthy. The rain was light at first and he thought it would soon stop, but it got heavier and turned into a downpour, very cold. He could have waited at some friendly house, but by that time he was already wet, and he decided, unwisely, that he should press on for home. A wetting when you are working, or even when you are walking, is unpleasant, but at least you can keep warm. Travelling by trap is another matter; the pony is wet, but warm, the driver gets colder as he gets wetter. He caught a bad cold. He tried to ignore it, but it didn't ignore him; by the week-end he had to give in. He hated being confined to the house, and worried about the weather and the crops that had still to be saved. Mam tried to calm and reassure him. 'You can tell the boys what they are to do, and you know you can depend on them,' she said, knowing as well as he knew that all his farming knowledge had been passed on to them and that they could be depended on without question. But he roamed from room to room, unable to be easy anywhere, became feverish, got in the way of the kitchen-work, but would not go to bed. But he had to give in eventually, and I think he must have known that he was much worse and that it was not simply a cold. The following day Mam sent for the doctor. I remember that when the doctor was leaving I was given the job of opening the lawn-gate for him and closing it after him. He stopped to say, 'Thank you, son,' and then stopped again a few yards on and called me. 'Do whatever your mother wants you to do. Be good to her and help her any way you can.' I didn't understand why he said that; after all it was Daddy who was sick, not Mam. Now I know it was because he knew what no one in our house knew, and because he was a kind man. Some time during that day I first heard the terrifying word Pneumonia.

He was cared for every minute of the day and night; if love and care could have saved him he would not have died, but we learned that love and care are not enough. He died on the 25th of September 1905, and was buried beside his son John, his little infant daughter, and our Frances.

Everything changed then for all of us in that sad house, but it was the most sad thing that ever happened to Mam, and wouldn't you think she would have got used to people dying and to losing members of her family? This was different; I suppose it was as if the whole world had slipped away from under her feet. Not long after the funeral I went into the dairy one day to get something or other and she was standing quite still by the window leaning on the table where she made the butter. She turned slowly and looked at me as if she didn't see me. I could see she had been crying and that wasn't like Mam at all – so sure, so competent, able for every situation. I thought she might be cross with me, but instead she held out her hands just as though she was asking me, without a word, to ... I don't know what ... and pulled me to her and held me. I felt her sobbing and I was embarrassed and sad, and I was too young to understand or to help.

It was in those dark days that I began to see that the life of our household had not revolved around my mother only, as I had supposed, but that it had been a happy partnership. She had married at the age of nineteen, and during the succeeding forty years had never been alone, cheered and re-assured by companionship and a sharing of responsibility. It was frighteningly clear to her that now she would have to stumble on as best she could, alone. She saw ahead only a bleak loneliness, never again the familiar face, never the familiar voice; there would be only the drudgery of days, the empty place, the weight of the many who depended on her, the long winter nights. She knew this and I think it broke her heart. That's a phrase we use without meaning it literally or expecting it to be understood so, and yet if by "heart" we mean "courage", it is true that my father's death broke her heart. She was never the same brave soul again; she lost her gallant spirit that accepted all, even the inevitability of pain, grief and loss; she had encountered all of these and had faced them down. All except that final blow. She lost then her joy in life, her certainty of good.

Was some of that joy lost to all of us when he died?

I find it very strange in thinking back, that of the two who died in that unforgotten year, when, I believe, I stopped being a child and had to start growing up, it was Rich that I missed at first more keenly. But as the years go by, it is the memory of that other one, that quiet man who had no words to explain himself, who was unfailingly kind to every member of his family gathered about him in his little kingdom, as indeed to everyone he ever met, it is the influence and example of that gentle man that have become part of my thinking and of my life.

Notes and Acknowledgments

'And all the spangled host keep watch in squadrons bright' is from 'On the Morning of Christ's Nativity' by John Milton.

The stories are presented more or less in order of being written, the earliest in the 1960s and in every decade since, the latest in 2014.

'The Heel of the Hunt' was published in New Irish Writing, *The Irish Press*, 3 August 1974 and in *Best Irish Short Stories* edited by David Marcus, Elek Books Ltd, London, 1976. It won the author a Hennessy Literary Award in 1975. 'Chapel Street' was published in New Irish Writing, *The Irish Press*, autumn 1977. 'The Long Consequences' was published in New Irish Writing, *The Irish Press*, c. 1982. 'Men of the World' and 'A Wild Goose' were published in New Irish Writing, *The Irish Press*, 6 February 1982. 'Dawn on the Boyne' started life in Irish as 'Brú na Bóinne'.

'Growing Up' is a longer version of the story 'Rich' and was written as a family memoir, not with publication in mind. It is set on the family farm in Ballygoman, outside Wexford town, between 1895 and 1905. The subject is the author's father, who was aged six to sixteen at this time.

The drawing on page 136 is by the author.